HARBINGERS 16

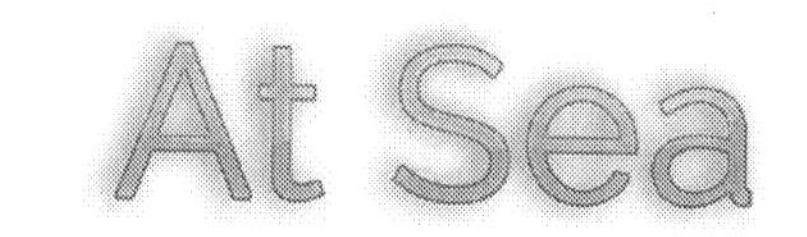

Alton Gansky

Bill Myers, Jeff Gerke,
and Angela Hunt

Published by Amaris Media International.

Cover Design: Angela Hunt
Photo credits: ©alexzaitsev-fotolia.com

ISBN-13: 978-1539557760
ISBN-10: 1539557766

For more information, visit us on Facebook:
https://www.facebook.com/pages/Harbingers/705107309586877

or *www.harbingersseries.com*.

HARBINGERS

A novella series by
Bill Myers, Jeff Gerke, Angela Hunt,
and Alton Gansky

IN THIS FAST-PACED world with all its demands, the four of us wanted to try something new. Instead of the longer novel format, we wanted to write something equally as engaging but that could be read in one or two sittings—on the plane, waiting to pick up the kids from soccer, or as an evening's read.

We also wanted to play. As friends and seasoned novelists, we thought it would be fun to create a game we could participate in together. The rules were simple:

Rule #1

Each of us will write as if we were one of the characters in the series:

Bill Myers will write as Brenda, the street-hustling tattoo artist who sees images of the future.

Jeff Gerke will write as Chad, the mind reader with devastating good looks and an arrogance to match.

Angela Hunt will write as Andi, the brilliant-but-geeky young woman who sees inexplicable patterns.

Alton Gansky will write as Tank, the naïve, big-hearted jock with a surprising connection to a healing power.

Rule #2

Instead of the four of us writing one novella

together (we're friends but not crazy), we would write it like a TV series. There would be an overarching storyline into which we'd plug our individual novellas, with each story written from our character's point of view.

If you're keeping track, this is the order:

Harbingers #1—*The Call*—Bill Myers
Harbingers #2—*The Haunt*ed—Frank Peretti
Harbingers #3—*The Sentinels*—Angela Hunt
Harbingers #4—*The Girl*—Alton Gansky

Volumes #1-4 omnibus: *Cycle One: Invitation*

Harbingers #5—*The Revealing*—Bill Myers
Harbingers #6—*Infestation*—Frank Peretti
Harbingers #7—*Infiltration*—Angela Hunt
Harbingers #8—*The Fog*—Alton Gansky

Volumes #5-8 omnibus: *Cycle Two: Mosaic*

Harbingers #9—*Leviathan*—Bill Myers
Harbingers #10—*The Mind Pirates*—Frank Peretti
Harbingers #11—*Hybrids*—Angela Hunt
Harbingers #12—*The Village*—Alton Gansky

Volumes 9-12 omnibus: *Cycle Three: The Probing*

Harbingers #13—*Piercing the Veil*—Bill Myers
Harbingers #14—*Home Base*—Jeff Gerke
Harbingers #15—*Fairy*—Angela Hunt
Harbingers #16—*At Sea*—Alton Gansky

There you have it, at least for now. We hope you'll find these as entertaining in the reading as we did in the writing.

Bill, Jeff, Angie, and Al

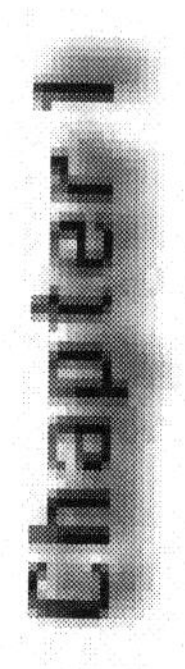

ALONE AGAIN, UNNATURALLY

ROCKING.

Like an infant in a cradle.

Gentle. Smooth. Even.

Then came a new sensation: Someone had been using my mouth as an ashtray. A vile film covered my tongue and teeth. Still, I wasn't ready to open my eyes. Mostly I just wanted to slip back into the blanket of sleep I had been living in a short time before.

Blanket? I could tell I lay upon a narrow bed but I felt no blanket over me. I was warm. Too warm. Only then did I risk opening an eye. The room was lit but only dimly. Missing was the harshness of an incandescent light. What I saw was natural illumination, enough to see but not read in comfortably.

I forced myself to take several deep breaths. The air was a tad stale and carried a hint of salt. I swung my legs over the side of the bed, buried my face in my hands and tried to focus my thoughts. It wasn't easy. My brain was filled with a thick London fog and my thoughts were as slippery as a sink full of eels.

Lowering my hands, I stared at the thin carpet on the floor. It was a perfectly acceptable beige, which somehow managed to look new and old at the same time. My brain fog lifted a little and I was capable of noticing something that shouldn't be: black, highly polished dress shoes—on my feet. The kind of shoes a man wore with a—

Tux.

Sure enough, I wore a pair of well-tailored tuxedo pants. I stood and touched my waist. Cummerbund. There was also a white shirt with posts instead of buttons, and a bowtie. I had been sleeping in a bowtie. The thing is, I hate tuxes. At least I think I do. Try as I might, I couldn't remember the last time I wore a tux, or why I was wearing one now.

Across the room was a full-length mirror that confirmed everything I had just discovered. I didn't need a mirror to tell me what I was wearing. I puzzled that out pretty quickly. What I *did* need was a mirror or something else to tell me who the guy in the reflection was. He looked familiar. Young and big. Extra big—six-foot-three maybe and tipping the scales at over 250 pounds. That was a guess, of course, but I didn't think I was far wrong. A little wide in the shoulders too. I stepped closer to the mirror and touched its cool, smooth surface. The reflection touched its side of the glass.

A man should recognize his own image, shouldn't he? Why couldn't I recognize mine?

My first question had been: Why am I sleeping in a tuxedo? That seemed like a small question now. What I really wanted to know was who I am. I also wouldn't mind knowing where I was. I didn't recognize anything in the cramped room.

"Well, this ain't right." At least my voice sounded familiar.

I rubbed my eyes until they hurt. Maybe I was still asleep and having one of those hyperreal dreams. I know a couple of people who dream in high-def and technicolor. It sounded cool to me, but they didn't think so. I guess dreams should be dreamy and not too realistic.

I bent forward and rested my hands on my knees. I wasn't feeling any too good. My stomach was in rebellion about something. The rocking of the floor? Somethin' I ate? I had no idea. I took a few minutes to will my stomach into submission then straightened again.

I took in my room: a single bed, made-up but rumpled where I had been dozing. A small dresser was opposite the bed and stood near the full-length mirror. A wood desk was tucked in one corner; the kinda desk you see in a hotel room.

Is that what this is? A hotel? A hotel with a rocking floor? That made no sense, but then nothing I saw or experienced since I crawled out of—maybe I should say *off* the sack—made any kinda sense.

The light in the room was pretty dim. A quick survey told me that no light bulbs were burning anywhere. The only source of illumination came from a wide but narrow window in the wall. I walked to it. It was set kinda high but I could still see through it without much effort.

Gray. Outside was gray. Gray sky. Gray fog. Gray sea. That last observation explained a lot. I was on a boat, maybe I should say a ship. I tried to think about that some. My thoughts, what few I could lay a mental hand on, were jumbled like a dropped deck of playing cards. Some cards were face up; others face down. Except I had no way of putting them in order. My thinking was as unsettled as my gut.

At least the sea, what I could see of the sea, was pretty calm. My belly was glad for that.

The scum in my mouth still tasted bad. My tongue and cheeks seemed lined with felt. I took a couple of deep breaths and moved to a narrow and short hallway, more of an entry area really, and saw two doors. One was slightly wider than the other. I assumed the wider door led to a hallway; the smaller door had to lead to a bathroom. I guess I should call it a "head." I opened the second door and enjoyed a moment of satisfaction that my assumption had been correct.

The head had the basics of any home bathroom but in a smaller form. There was a glass-enclosed shower to one side. Clearly, it hadn't been designed for a man of my dimensions. If I wanted to get clean inside that thing I would have to soap the walls and spin around in it. That didn't matter now; I was more interested in evicting the taste in my mouth. I paid little attention to the toilet although I was sure I might be more interested in it should my stomach turn traitor.

The sink was smaller than what I would expect and it looked a little out of date. As I thought about it, I could say the same thing for the whole room I had just been in and the rest of the bathroom.

I turned the faucet handle looking for a nice stream of cold water. I got nuthin'. I mean nuthin'.

"Great. Jus' great."

I tried the hot water handle. Again, a great big nuthin'. Maybe the valves below the sink had been cranked shut. No idea why that might be, but I wanted to check. To do so, I needed more light. A man didn't need much light to drink a little water and splash his face a bit, but more than that would require a bit more illumination.

I flipped the light switch and was once again denied. I tried flipping the switch a few times as if I could annoy it into working. No dice.

"All right then, let's try this." I turned on the shower. Well, I tried to turn it on. No water there.

Of course, there was the toilet, but there was no water in the basin, not that I would gargle with it if there were. Now I was getting irritated.

With a mouth that sported a film that tasted like the inside of an old rain gutter, I left the head and exited the room. It was time to find someone to listen to my rants.

The corridor was empty. No passengers strolling to or from rooms. No cleaning crew changing out towels and running vacuum cleaners. No children barreling down the hallway like they were in a human demolition derby. Just a twilight dark and lots and lots of quiet.

That last observation made me wonder. If this was a ship at sea—and the ocean outside my window pretty much convinced me of that—then shouldn't I be hearing the rumble of mighty engines? Perhaps we were still tied up to the dock. After all, I could only look out one side of the boat.

Still, the boat rocked a little and I didn't think cruise ships did that when tied to a pier. But what did I know? Not much. I had a fuzzy brain, and a scummy mouth, and no memory of the past beyond the moment I woke up on the bed.

I walked through the gloom. What little light there was came from a window at the end of the hall. Sconces were spaced evenly along the walls but not one offered any light. They were pretty and useless.

The light at the end of the corridor drew me closer. Light was better than growing twilight. I walked slowly, feeling a little wobbly as if I had been on an all-night bender. That couldn't be. I had only been drunk once in my life and have avoided alcohol ever since…

That was a memory. Why would I remember that and not my own name? Maybe that was a good sign. Maybe not. My confusion grew. The more I reached for a memory, the more difficult it became to think. Maybe I was having a stroke.

Could that be? A stroke? Probably not. My reflection said I was young. Maybe young guys could have strokes, but I didn't think that was common.

Besides, I seemed to be able to think in complete sentences.

I stopped. "Peter Piper picked a peck of pickled peppers." That came out just fine, so the stroke idea seemed unlikely. I shook my head. What did I know? Would a man with a stroke know if he his speech sounded right?

My head was beginning to hurt.

"A concussion. That might be it." My voice rolled down the corridor. Those words brought an odd sensation. I had known people with concussions. I couldn't name one person, but the realization felt right.

"I gotta get some help." I didn't need to say that out loud, but hearing my own voice brought a little comfort.

Twenty-five or thirty steps later I reached the window at the end of the corridor. It was about three feet wide and five feet or so tall. The glass was clear but spotted with watermarks. The view outside showed a thick, wet fog. The ocean was flat and two shades grayer. I looked both left and right and saw no sign of a port. "Definitely at sea."

Below—I guessed I was three stories or so above the deck below—was the front end of the ship. The deck looked smooth and appeared to be something like concrete, not wood slats. What I didn't see were people. Where were the people? Even on a gray day like today, people should be strolling the deck. My attitude was turning as gray as the fog.

The fog bothered me. For some reason, the sight of it gave me the willies, like something might be hiding in the mist. A shiver ran through me as if someone had dumped a barrel of ice water over my head.

I turned my back to the window. To my right was a wide ornamental metal stairway. One side of it went up, the other went down. I chose the steps going down. Why? Can't tell ya. I just did. My hope was that I'd find someone who could direct me to the ship's doctor, and if not a someone, then a sign.

Halfway down the staircase an awful thought occurred to me. Maybe there was no doctor onboard. I hadn't seen anyone else, why should I believe there was a doctor?

There was only one way to find out.

A BRIDGE TOO NEAR

I WAS FEELING a tad lonely. Was I the kinda guy who was prone to loneliness? I guessed no, but what did I know? At that moment, not much. For all I knew, I might be an emotional cripple. If I was, then this amnesia might be a good thing.

The cause of my loneliness was pretty easy to figure out. I had come to in a room alone. I had searched the ship from the main deck up and saw no one. I called out for help but no one answered. The gray fog was a downer, too. I couldn't see a horizon in the distance, or lights from a city. There was no sun or moon in the sky, just a dull, eerie canopy of mist. When I looked over the rail I couldn't help but notice that the sea was gray, too. For some reason, that didn't surprise me. Not a bit.

I had emerged from the stairway—I think they call it a companionway on a ship (but again, what do I know?)—onto a wide deck. A wide, *empty* deck. I could see almost to the front of the boat and all the way to the back. Nobody. I walked to the back, peeking into every window I came across. I saw nobody. I saw no light. I saw no proof that anyone was onboard. Of course, I hadn't searched the whole ship, but why would this deck be empty of people? The ship was clearly a cruise ship, although it seemed like it was a generation or two older than modern craft. The doorknobs looked old. And the stateroom doors used real, honest-to-goodness keys to lock and unlock them, not those magnetic or chip keycards.

That thought made me realize something. I could remember some things like being in a hotel, several different hotels, but I couldn't remember why. My Swiss cheese brain seemed willing to let some information through, but nothing about me. Seemed a bit unfair.

As I walked to the rear of the boat I read every sign I came across. I was looking for one the said, SHIPS DOCTOR, or MEDICAL, or YOU HAVE ENTERED THE TWILIGHT ZONE. No luck. What signs I did find directed me to decks with odd names like "Promenade," or "Lido," and several that pointed the way to the life boats.

When I reached the stern I found an open area with lounge chairs neatly arranged in rows, a few patio-like tables, and two spas. There was also a bar, but no bartender. The bar was fully stocked. "It's a shame that I'm not a drinker—"

And there it was: another bit of random information about myself. I had nothing to tie the thought to. It just popped into my head. "At this rate, I'll know everything about myself in a couple of years."

My voice sounded slightly off. Kinda muted, like the air was muffling the sound. Didn't matter. I was going to talk to myself until I found someone else to talk to.

I had another reason for moving aft. When I first looked out the window of my room, or whoever's room I had been in, I got the sense that we weren't under power. The lack of lights made that seem like a real possibility. I now had proof. There was no wake. A ship this size should leave a sizeable wake no matter how slow it was moving.

We—I—was adrift.

Alone.

In the middle of nowhere.

Going nowhere.

Now I really wanted a little company.

I looked over the railing and into the gray water thirty or so feet below. From this height, a jumper would get a pretty nasty sting. I waited for the urge to end it all to come over me. It didn't. That would just be stupid. "Can't get into heaven if you die stupid." I doubted there was any solid theology in that thought, but it gave me a tiny reason to smile.

I figured it was time to get back to my search. I was no longer focused on finding a doctor. Aside from the nasty taste in my mouth, I felt fine.

Befuddled, sure, and more than a little confused, but physically I felt tiptop.

Before I committed to searching the right side of the deck, I helped myself to a soda from behind the bar. I'd pay for it later if I found someone to pay. I used the soda to rinse out my mouth. It did the trick.

From there I moved up the other side of the main deck doing the same thing I had done on the left side. The word *starboard* rose in my brain. "Starboard means the right side of a boat; port means the left." Why would I know that? Was I a sailor? Maybe I was one of the crew.

I shook my head as if doing so would dislodge a few more nuggets of memory. No such luck. I probably had just learned the terms from a book or a movie or somethin'. Still, it could mean my brain was gainin' some traction.

My starboard side stroll was as useless as the port side. When I reached the bow I began to despair. Despair is fine, I guess, as long as you don't give into it. Nothing to do now except move higher or search the lower decks. I chose to go up. Surely, I told myself, someone will have to be on the bridge. No sailor would let a ship drift at sea.

The bridge overlooked the bow and was several stair climbs higher than the main deck. All the better to see the sea, I figured.

The bridge had been easy to find and to my surprise its door stood wide open. I crossed the threshold. I entered slowly, not sure if I was allowed to enter the brain center of a cruise ship.

It appeared that I had been wrong; apparently sailors would leave the bridge empty. This didn't sit well with me. So far I held out some hope that others were onboard and I would find them sooner or later. I had doubts before; now I had serious doubts.

I studied the controls long enough to know that I had never been an officer on a cruise ship. I had no clues what the chrome handles and levers did. I did notice that there was no ship's wheel. Instead there was something like a podium with several blank screens and a coupla things that looked like controllers for a video game.

There were other monitors spread around the bridge, all of them tucked in a U-shaped console that filled most of the floor space. It looked like something out of some sci-fi movie. If I didn't feel so confused and alone, I might have appreciated all the high-tech stuff. As it was, I felt only disappointment.

There were two leather seats centered in the room and facing the front of the bridge. I assumed one was for the captain. Between the chairs was a console of gauges and small computer monitors—all dead. There was also a microphone. I doubted that a ship dead in the water without enough power to switch on a light would have an active intercom system or radio.

Still I had to try. After all, I could be wrong.

I wasn't.

A pair of binoculars rested in the captain's chair. I took them. I used them. All I saw was a deep shade of gray in every direction.

Mounted to one wall was a "pigeon hole" case, the kind of cabinet in which a person might keep rolls of plans. Not plans, charts. I was a little confused because the ship's bridge was clearly high-tech even if it was as dead as a stone. Why have paper charts?

"Emergencies?"

I didn't answer myself. The why didn't matter. If those were charts, then I might at least get an idea where I was.

I grabbed several rolls. Beneath the cabinet was a table just the right size for the wide paper. I unrolled one. Yep. Charts. Sea charts. It showed sea lanes and nearby land with ports.

I didn't recognize a single thing. The names of the ports meant nuthin' to me. Place names: nuthin'. I saw a few islands. Nuthin'. Even if I could recognize a place or two, it would do me little good. I had no idea which chart was the right one. There were at least twenty rolls.

"Nuts."

I re-rolled the charts and put them back where I found them. I don't know why. There wasn't anyone around to yell at me.

I took several deep breaths and tried to clear my mind of depression and doubt. I'll admit that I was tempted to sit in the captain's chair and just wait, and wait, and wait. But that passed in a few moments. My gut told me that I wasn't the kinda guy who liked to sit around and wait for things to happen.

"If answers won't come to me, then I'll hunt them down."

OUT OF THE CLOSET

DECISIONS NEEDED TO be made, even if they were wrong. So far, everything I had seen made me think I was the last soul onboard a powerless, drifting cruise ship. I felt alone but I hadn't proved it. Since I was still aboard, there might be other people snoozin' in their bunks dressed in tuxes or some other kinda fancy dress. I had no proof of that. Of course, I had no proof I was wrong. Bottom line: I had spent the better part of an hour searching the topside of the ship and knew less than when I started. Maybe the answers lay below decks. After all, that's where all this began for me.

I left the bridge and made my way back to the main deck. I was gonna take another quick look around when I noticed something that had got by me during my first search. Aside from gazing at the fog that surrounded the *SS Twilight Zone* and the ocean below, all my attention had been turned on the rooms and the deck. That's where the people should be. This time I forced myself to broaden my gaze. In some ways I wish I hadn't.

Spaced along the deck just inside the safety rail were cranes—davits. They were ten feet tall or so and shaped like steel candy canes. A metal cable ran from the base of the davit and up the steel pole, along the crook, hung free over the side of the ship and hovered about five feet above the water. A device on the end the cable was clearly meant to attach to something—something that was no longer there.

"Lifeboats."

My words chilled my blood. I walked the length of the deck examining every davit. The davits were used in pairs, a lifeboat meant to be hangin' between them. Not anymore. There wasn't a life boat to be found. That meant…

"Not good. Not good by a long shot."

The pit of my stomach became a runaway elevator. If it had been possible, it would have crawled out of me and jumped overboard.

The ship had been abandoned.

And I had been left behind.

It shouldn't have been possible, but I now felt twice as lonely as before and I was pretty doggone lonely to begin with.

I circled the main deck again this time searching the sea. Maybe the life boats could still be seen and if they were, then I could… could… I had no idea what I could do in that situation. Still, I strained my vision trying to peer through the fog looking for an emergency beacon or the shape of a boat that could hold a couple dozen people. I had counted the davits and my guess was that the ship carried twenty-five lifeboats. The ship was much smaller than the big monsters I had seen in pictures. Ships with many decks above the main deck and many below. The kinda ship that carried a few thousand passengers. Perhaps that was one of the reasons I thought of the ship as old. It seemed small.

Still, this boat, it seemed to me, could carry several hundred passengers. Maybe even a thousand or more.

I let those thoughts go. They didn't matter at the moment. I had a long way to go before I reached the goal line.

Once I had confirmed that no life boats were near enough to see or hear, I continued on with my plan. I had to. I had no other plan to follow.

Two thoughts rattled around in my head, each wanting attention. One was a sense of sadness. Life boats would have their own source of power, working engines, and radios. The other was a question: What could make the captain and crew abandon ship?

I had no answer and I had a strong feeling that if I found one, I wouldn't like it.

MY PLAN WAS simple. I would search the ship by brute force. Based on the image provided by the mirror in my room—if was really my room—I was a brute force kinda guy. Maybe that was true; maybe it wasn't. For now, I was going to embrace it as the truth. I began one level down. The same level I had been on when I came to.

Maybe there was a better way of doing this, but if there was, then I couldn't see it. I began banging on stateroom doors. I also exercised my lungs a lot.

"Hello? Anybody there? Hello?"

Door after door and always the same silence.

There was another problem. I had seen a placard with a drawing of the ship in cross section. Kinda one of those, "You are here," things. I doubted that I was any kinda rocket scientist, but I knew the deeper in the ship I went, the darker it would get. With no power, I would be descending into a crypt.

Great. My own thoughts are creeping me out. Like I need more creeping out.

I reached the end of the first corridor and found an in-wall cabinet with a glass front. Inside was a fire hose and, praise God, a flashlight. It was a big one, too. I'm sure it was meant for crew in times of emergency, but I decided to help myself anyway.

I broke the glass which gave me access to a lever that unlocked the cabinet door. I took the light. I flicked it on and it came to life.

"Finally, something good."

I went level by level deeper and deeper into the ship. Some of the levels were below the waterline. I anticipated that and my love for my new flashlight grew.

The beam of light splashed on the walls, ceiling, and floor. If I tripped now it would be because of stupidity or carelessness, not because I was strolling in the dark.

I continued banging on doors and calling for attention. I continued to get nothing in return. It reminded me of a flashlight scene from the old *X-Files* television show.

Four decks down from where I started, I heard it. I had stopped to take a breather and to rest the hand I had been using to pound on hard wood doors. It was a soft sound. At first it seemed too distant, but then nearer.

No words. Muffled.

Weeping.

A deep weeping. Not a child. Not a woman.

I closed my eyes and tried to turn up the sensitivity in my ears. A man. Somewhere a man was weeping. It broke my heart.

I moved slowly and with soft steps, like a cat sneaking up on prey. At each doorway I paused and placed an ear near the door. The weeping grew louder. A dozen doors later I located the right room. Well, not a room. It was a closet of some kind. A sign on the door read: CREW ONLY.

I took a few deep breaths and willed myself to move slowly. Whoever was inside the closet was definitely upset and I didn't want to scare the life out of the guy. I was pretty sure that he, like me, was having a really bad day.

I tapped on the door. "Hey buddy, you okay?"

The weeping stopped. I heard a scuffling sound like someone scampering away from the door.

"It's okay, man. I'm a friend."

No response.

"You mind if I open the door?"

"It's locked." The voice sounded fairly young. Adult, but not old.

"Can you unlock it for me?"

"Do you think I'd still be in here if I could unlock it? Don't be dense. It's locked from the outside."

I was beginning to get an idea about why someone might lock the guy up. He wasn't very warm and fuzzy.

"You know something, pal. You and me might be the only two people on this tub. It might be wise to make a friend instead of an enemy."

I heard mumbling. "Yeah. Okay. Right. I'm a little upset."

"Understandable. I'm a bit off my game, too." I studied the door. "Okay, I'm gonna try the doorknob. That okay with you?"

"I already told you it was locked."

"Then it won't hurt anything for me to give it a try. I'm just givin' you a heads up." I gave the knob the once over. It had a place for a key, which made sense to me. I'd expect a room reserved for crew might need to be locked. Still, I gave the brass knob a twist. It didn't cooperate.

"Believe me now?"

Grumpy was getting on my nerves and I didn't have many nerves left.

"And I told you it wouldn't hurt to try—and it didn't." Deep breath. "I don't know how much room you have in there. Can you back away from the door?"

"Yes." I heard shuffling, then, "Well?"

"Well what?"

"I'm out of the way. Do whatever you were going to do."

"Oh, sorry. My X-ray vision isn't working." I was certain I could get the guy out, but every time he opened his mouth I felt an urge to leave him right where he was.

I took a step back, raised a foot and kicked the door just to the side of the doorknob. It rattled a little but stayed put. This would have been so much easier if I wasn't wearing a monkey suit and dress shoes.

"That's it?" The stranger's voice pressed through the door. "That's your great plan?"

I kicked the door again. I kicked harder than I should and felt pleasure in the exertion. I also felt some pleasure at seeing a chunk of the door with the knob splinter and fall to the deck. The door swung in with an earsplitting crash.

A blur of a man flew out of the closet like an iron ball out of a canon and rammed me in the chest with his shoulder. I back-peddled, surprised by the attack. Then he had his hands around my throat, his fingers squeezing and squeezing. The good news was he wasn't very strong. Still, it was enough to make me drop my flashlight.

The temptation was to grab his wrists and pull his arms down. I didn't. Instead, I raised a hand between his extended arms and took hold of his face. I clamped down—hard. He screamed, so I assumed I had his attention. I didn't wait for retaliation; I brought a quick knee to his gut striking him just about belt high.

Air left his lungs. His arms dropped. He wobbled. It was a good time for me to seize his belt in my right hand, lift, and shove him in the chest with my left. He hit the deck on his back, just as I intended. That was when the war in my brain started. Part of my mind wanted me to kill the little twerp; another part just wanted me to beat on him for a bit; and about half by brain was tugging hard on my reins. Lucky for Grumpy, I felt inclined to follow my more reasonable self. Truth is, I felt like something or someone was holding me back.

I picked up my flashlight. "Are we done?" I watched him roll on the deck for a few moments. "I can do this all day."

He raised a hand. "I know when I'm beat." He sucked in a barrel full of air. "Did you have to kick me so hard?"

"I pulled that kick, buddy. It coulda been worse, much worse. Besides, I seem to recall your hands around my neck." That's when I noticed his right arm. It sported a dragon tattoo that looked very familiar.

"Sorry about that." He stopped rolling around but spent a few more moments moaning. "I thought you were someone else."

"Best I can tell, pal, we're the only two people around."

"It's not people that worry me."

I didn't know what to make out of that. Maybe he hit his head when I put him on the floor.

"What's your name?"

He gazed at the ceiling. "I don't know."

"At least we have that in common." I extended my hand to him. "Need help getting up?"

He shook his head. "I can manage."

He rolled over and pushed himself up until he was on all fours and made several attempts to stand, but couldn't quite manage it.

"Okay, maybe I could use an assist."

I grabbed an arm and lifted him to his feet. He swayed a little, then looked at me.

"You're a big one, aren't you?"

He was young, looked in pretty good shape, and had the kind of looks girls seemed to go for. He wore a formal white shirt, the kind with ruffles over the buttons. Like me, he wore tuxedo pants and dress shoes. No jacket, though. I imagined that it was in the corner of the closet. His shirt sleeves were rolled up. "That's some tattoo. Where'd you get that?"

He looked at his arm. "I don't know. I don't remember much."

That I understood. I moved to the closet and shone my light in. It didn't take long for me to recognize a simple janitor's closet.

"How did you get stuck in here?"

"Don't be an idiot. I didn't get stuck. I was imprisoned."

I let the insult pass. "Okay then, who imprisoned you?"

"My dad."

"Your dad locked you in the closet? I take it he's never parent of the year."

He looked at me with an odd mix of anger and sorrow. It was kinda heartbreaking.

"Where's your dad now?"

"He's dead."

I didn't like the sound of this. "He died on the boat?"

"No, he's been dead for a while."

"How could he… Never mind. Let me ask you something. Do I look familiar to you?"

"You hitting on me, big guy?"

That did it. "If you don't shut that smart mouth of yours, I'll be hitting on you, but not in the way you think."

A wave of guilt washed over me. He just stared at me, looking a little like a scolded puppy. The guy could switch from mean-spirited to the verge of tears in a heartbeat. I felt sorry for him. It also made me think he might be a little unhinged.

"Sorry." I gave a little shrug. "It looks like we've both had a rough day. I'm a little edgy. What say we start over?" I extended my hand. "I'd introduce myself to you but—you know—I have that whole amnesia thing going on."

Grumpy nodded and took my hand. "Same here."

Then the ship shuddered.

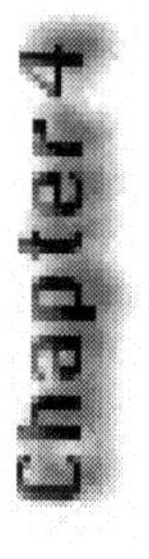

SHUFFLING THE DECKS

I HAD BEEN just about to ask him how his dead father could lock him in a closet when he disappeared. In fact, the whole hallway vanished. Gray light surrounded me, which meant I had somehow made it back to one of the upper decks. The problem was, I hadn't planned to go back to the upper decks.

Something else was different. I was no longer on my feet. I was on my hands and knees, swaying like a drunk dog. I didn't feel any too good, either. I proved that point by emptying my stomach on the deck. I hadn't puked in years. I don't know. Maybe I had and just couldn't remember it.

Once I was done decorating the deck with my last meal, I tipped over onto my side, then my back and waited to see if more retching was to come.

Slow breaths. Even breaths. Relax. It will pass.

The nausea did pass, but my stomach continued to cramp a little longer. When I opened my eyes I saw the fog-shrouded sky again, except it was different somehow. A different shade of gray. And brighter.

"There you are."

A familiar voice. Grumpy's voice.

He had more to say. "Now, that was weird. I mean off the charts weird—eww." He pointed at the deck. "Did you do that?"

"Of course not, I just like to find a puddle of puke and lay down next to it." I sat up and wrapped my arms around my knees. I took a few more deep breaths praying that I wouldn't puke again—especially in front of Grumpy.

"To each his own, I guess."

"I was kidding. Yes, I'm responsible for the mess. Apparently being snapped from one place on a ship to another upsets my tummy."

"Tummy? Really? What are you, six years old?"

I struggled to my feet and tried to look even taller.

Grumpy raised his hands. "Okay, okay. Just trying to be friendly."

"You don't have many friends do you, smart mouth?"

"How would I know? I'm as blank as you. Well, maybe I'm not that blank, but I have the same memory affliction you do. Remember?"

"Let me guess. That's supposed to be a joke."

"Nope, but I've got to admit, it was clever." He walked to the rail. "I have a point to make."

"Yeah? And what's that?" I joined him at the rail and noticed another difference. The ocean was green and a little choppy. Still, I could tell the ship was dead in the water.

"First, see if you have a handkerchief in that tux of yours. It's difficult enough looking at you as it is. The addition of vomit dribbles makes it worse."

As if I wasn't already embarrassed enough. Turns out, I did have a handkerchief in the inside breast pocket of my coat. I used it as requested.

"Why are we in tuxes?"

He shrugged. "One mystery at a time, Big Guy. First, I have a question or two, assuming you're done spewing."

"Let it go, pal. What's your question?"

"What's the first thing you remember?"

I gave that some thought. "You mean today?"

He looked at me like green ooze was coming outta my ears. "Can you remember anything before today?"

"No, I told you… Okay, I get the point." I looked at the soiled cloth in my hand, then tossed it overboard. It wasn't the kind of thing that becomes a keepsake. "I remember waking up on the bed in my stateroom, or someone's stateroom."

"You were in bed?"

"No. I was *on* the bed. Fully dressed. Shoes and everything."

"Tell me everything from that point on."

"First, I have a question. Whatever happened back there put me on the deck and made me sick, yet you look unfazed. What's the deal?"

He smiled. I was surprised he knew how. "Didn't bother me a bit. In fact, it seemed kind of familiar." His smiled widened. "Don't hate me because I'm rugged."

Since arguing seemed the least productive thing to do, I caved and told him how I had come to in the stateroom, my search of the upper decks, and how I found him. He nodded.

"Is anything different now?"

"Yeah, I was transported from one of the lower decks back up here. That's pretty different."

He looked disappointed in me. "I mean different from what you saw before."

"The sea is green. Before it was gray."

"Anything else?"

"I haven't looked around since..." I motioned to the mess on the deck.

"So the sea is a different color?"

"Yep. And it is a little more active. Choppy."

"Uh-huh." He raised a hand to his face and tapped his lips with his index finger.

"Uh-huh what?"

"Try to stay with me on this—"

"Do you have to be so condescending?"

"Ooooh, that's a big word."

"One you don't seem to understand." My temper was swelling. "I could throw you over this rail, you know."

Grumpy shook his head. "No, you can't. It's not in you. You're not that kind of guy. You're one of those gentle giants."

"I wasn't gentle when I put you on the deck a short time ago."

"Yes you were, Big Guy. You could've beat me into a pile of goo, but you didn't. You took care of business. That's a fact and I have the bruises to prove it. You even apologized to me. Thugs don't do that."

My head was starting to ache. I don't think I could beat this guy in a battle of wits. He was mouthy, annoying, self-centered. I learned that in less than ten minutes with him. In addition to all of that, he seemed to be hiding a brilliant brain behind his barbs.

When he did speak, he carried on as if he were lecturing a class. "First, my memory goes back about as far as yours, but while you were trying to figure out how to open the door to the hallway, I was being locked in a closet by my dead father."

"I know how to work a door… I been meaning to ask you about that whole dead father thing."

"Not now. First things first. Our memories go back about the same amount of time. Have your forgotten anything since you awoke on the bed?"

I gave that some thought. "I don't think so, but then again, how would I know what I forgot?"

He looked disappointed in me. "Gaps, Big Guy. Gaps. You just described a moment by moment sequence of all that happened since you woke up, right? Any gaps in that story? Did you come up on deck, then find yourself in the galley or some other place?"

"No."

"Okay, that's good. It means that our brains are still working the way they're supposed to. Well, mine is anyway."

"That water looks awful cold, dude."

He raised a hand. "Sorry, apparently I'm not a very nice guy."

"I get that feeling. Where ya goin' with this?"

"The fact that we can remember anything tells us something about our problem. Our memory loss isn't from brain damage. We can remember, just not past a certain point. We can talk intelligently…well, I at least—"

"You really want to test your theory about me being a nice guy?"

"Nah. I don't see that ending well for me. Besides, we need to work together. My point is this: I feel a little groggy, but not so much that I can't reason. You too?"

"Yeah, but my brain is clearing as time passes. No important memories, but at least my thoughts aren't crashing into each other anymore."

He nodded. "That's a good thing. We're not brain damaged, but something is interfering with our ability to recall events prior to just a few hours ago. And what are the odds that two people would have the same affliction at the same time on the same boat and both be dressed in tuxes? You see what that means."

"I think so."

"There's a good chance we've been drugged. Probably something in our food."

"How do you figure that?"

"The tuxes, Big Guy. We're both wearing tuxes. And where do guys wear tuxes?"

"You mean like a banquet or something."

Again a nod. "On the nose. Right on the nose." He stepped away from the rail and walked to the spot where I tossed my cookies. "Look here."

"You want to study my vomit?"

"Why not? Vomitus can reveal a lot. You're not queasy are you?"

"Since I just vomited all over the deck, I guess you could say yes."

"Ah, point taken." He looked at the vile goop. "Anyway, I can tell you that you ate not many hours ago, so you could have ingested some drug."

"Why would anyone do that to me? To us?"

"I have no idea." He stepped back to the rail.

"Did they poison all the passengers?"

"I can't know that. Not yet anyway."

Thoughts began to bubble in my brain. "Did you notice that all the life boats are gone?"

He looked up and down the deck. "I haven't had a chance to look around, but you seem to be right. That means that we were rendered unconscious, had our memories stripped away, then were left behind while the crew and passengers took off in the life boats. Rude, if you ask me."

Rude wasn't the word for it. "Okay, smart guy. How did we get transported from the lower decks to the main deck?"

"How? No clue. But you said the fog is a different shade of gray, and that the sea is a different color. Right?"

"Yes, and it feels warmer now."

"I don't think we were transported up here. I think that was a consequence of something else. I think the whole ship was moved from one place to another."

"Like where?" I wasn't sure I wanted to know, but knowing was better than blind ignorance.

"I have no way of knowing."

I looked over the green sea. "You know what strikes me as odd?"

"I would think that all of this strikes you as odd."

"It does, but somehow I don't feel surprised. It's almost familiar. In a way, I'm surprised by my lack of surprise."

A moment of silence passed between us. "I suppose you think that's clever."

"It's the best I can do at the moment," I said. "Come on."

"Where are we going?"

"To look for others."

He frowned. "What makes you think you can find anyone else?"

"I found you, Grumpy. If I hadn't, you'd still be in a closet weeping. Now let's go before everything shifts again."

"Okay, but I want a different nickname. Grumpy isn't doing it for me."

"Whatever you say, Grumpy."

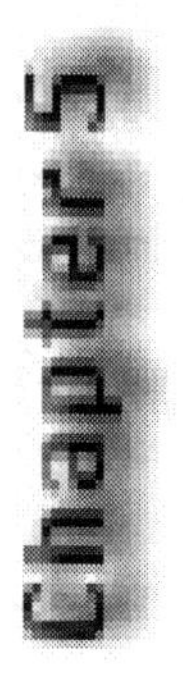

JUST BECAUSE YOU DON'T BELIEVE IN GHOSTS

THE CLOSET WAS the logical place to start. After all, it's where we left off when the ship shuffled or whatever it did.

"Let me get this right," Grumpy said. "You want us to start another search from this spot because it was as far as you got last time."

"You got it. It's only logical." Based on his tone, I figured he had a different opinion.

"Think about it, Big Guy."

"What?" I retrieved my flashlight.

"Just give it some thought. It's about time you gave thinking a go."

We were standing outside the now-broken door that had held Grumpy prisoner a short time ago. I looked at the closet. I looked at him and narrowed my eyes. Then I looked at the closet once more.

He held up his hands like a crook surrendering to the cops. "Okay, okay. Maybe that was a little harsh."

I couldn't have locked him in the closet if I wanted to, and I didn't really want to. Even if I did, I had busted up the part of the door with a knob. That door wouldn't be locked again anytime soon.

I leaned against one of the walls. "Okay, genius, what am I missing?"

"Last time we were here, what happened?"

"We ended up on the upper deck."

"Yep, with you puking all over—"

"I know what I was doing. I was the one doing it." This guy had a way of pushing my buttons. I was starting to regret finding him.

A half-sec later I realized what he was getting at. "You're saying if there are other people on board they could have been transported, shuffled, whatever into a room I've already checked."

"Bingo! Give the man a cigar."

That was disheartening. So what should I do? Start over? "You might be right, but let's assume you're not. We start from here and keep working our way down."

"I don't see the logic."

"It's simple. This is where we are right now, so this is where we pick up the search." I started down the corridor banging on doors, calling out, and jiggling doorknobs. All the doors were locked and no one replied to my calls.

We made it through the hall with me doing all the work and Grumpy following behind with a dog-eatin'-red-heart grin. I was beginning to question the guy's sanity. He might not be crazy, but he was pushing me in that direction.

We made our way down a level and started the whole process all over again. After banging on what I guessed was the twentieth stateroom on this deck, something caught my eye. Someone—no—something was standing at the end of the corridor. I raised my flashlight and aimed it down the corridor. The thing looked human-ish, stood at least seven feet tall, was pale, and if I was reading its expression correctly, a little put out about something.

Grumpy squeaked something, but my attention was on the thing at the end of the hall. It seemed I had three choices: turn and flee (I kinda liked that one); stay put and see what it did; or march up to it and see what it would do. I chose the last option. Don't ask why. It just seemed the kind of thing I would do.

I took a step forward. "Um, excuse me."

Grumpy almost choked. "What? You say *excuse me* to that thing? Are you planning on asking directions or something?"

I kept walking at a slow pace. No need to spook the ...spook. The odd thing was that all this seemed almost normal. I shoulda jumped outta my skin, but I didn't. Don't get me wrong, I was apprehensive enough for ten people, but I was shocked. Shouldn't I be shocked? I mean how often does a guy share an empty ship with a ghostly thingamajig?

"What are you doing?" Right behind me, Grumpy seemed terrified enough for both of us.

"I have no idea." I kept moving forward. My heart had turned into a jackhammer. If it beat any harder, it would break a rib or two.

As I drew closer I could see more detail; detail I didn't want to see. Its eyes were about the size of tennis balls. Fortunately, it had only the two eyes. *Be thankful for small things.* Its mouth was too wide for what passed for its face. It had lips: chapped, puffy, bloody looking lips. I prayed I was wrong about the bloody part. The thing's skin was pale, almost see-through and looked like someone had too little skin to offer so he stretched what little he had.

It wore clothes: torn, tattered, covered in something. I had no interest in knowing what. It stood on bare feet. I have big feet, but this thing made me look tiny.

Grumpy cleared his throat. "Um, listen Big Guy—"

"Hush. I'm trying to concentrate."

"Yeah, but—"

"Feel free to hang back. Or run. Whatever."

To Grumpy's credit, he stayed with me. Maybe he wasn't so smart after all.

When we were about fifteen feet from the visitor, it turned and fled down the side corridor. Of course I chased it. It seemed the thing to do. Chasing running people seemed normal for me, but I doubted I had ever chased a ghost or a zombie or an alien or whatever. At least that I could remember.

It took only three good strides for me to reach the end of the corridor and turn in the direction of the thing. It was gone. There was a stairway a short distance down the abutting corridor, but I had doubts about the thing's ability to reach them and disappear that fast.

"Okay," Grumpy said, "I'm going on record as being totally creeped out."

I turned. "Let me ask you something, buddy. Have you ever seen anything like that before?"

"Not exactly. My father looked pretty terrible, though."

"Your dead father that locked you in the closet?"

"Yep. That's the guy." He looked at me. "Don't stare at me that way. Just because you don't believe in ghosts doesn't mean there aren't any."

"That thing looked more like a demon than a ghost."

He cocked an eyebrow. "Seen many demons, have you?"

"Says the guy who sees his dead father."

He opened his mouth to say something, probably something snide and deserving of a fist to the nose, but he didn't. He closed his mouth.

I looked down the corridor again. "Back to my question. When you first saw that thing, did it seem a weird thing to see, or did it seem like you've seen things like that in the past?"

"What difference…" His eyes shifted from side to side a few times. The guy was thinking. "I see where you're going with this. No, it didn't seem abnormal. It scared me all right. I'm still scared."

"I had the same feeling: more of a *not again* than *this can't be possible*. Know what I mean?"

"Yeah, I know. What I don't know is why we would react that way."

I scratched my head. "I ain't got a clue. Not about that thing, not about this ship, not about why we can't remember."

"Hello?"

A voice.

"Anybody there?"

A woman's voice.

THE BLACK LADY AND THE REDHEAD

SHE STOOD AT the top of the stairs. The same staircase the bogyman had used to escape us. I couldn't tell if he left outta fear (doubtful) or just because he couldn't be bothered with such puny beings like us.

The woman held a flashlight, which told me that she had been hanging around on the lower decks. I aimed my flashlight at her. She returned the favor. I let my beam linger on her face for a moment, then lowered it. Her beam in my face made it hard to see, so I assumed my light was doing the same to her.

Once I moved the beam off her face and lowered it to her shoulders, she did the same for me.

Before me, at the top of the stairs, was a youngish black woman with dreadlocks. Her face made me think that she had seen some hard things in her life. She wore an evening dress, but no shoes. My guess was that women's heels weren't all that good for wandering around a ghost ship.

"Who are you?" Her tone was hard like steel and had an edge to it. To be honest, she scared me some.

"Really, lady? That's your question?" At least Grumpy was consistently rude to men and women.

"Don't mess with me, pretty boy. I ain't in a good mood."

"Clearly," Grumpy said.

I shone my light in his face. "Maybe you should let me do the talking."

"Why?"

"Because you have a tendency to make people hate you."

He pushed the flashlight away. "You're blinding me, moron."

I moved the light back up the stairwell and addressed the stranger. "That's the problem, ma'am. We don't know who we are, or where we are. We don't have any answers."

"You don't know who you are? You expect me to believe that?"

"Do you know who *you* are?" Grumpy said.

She didn't answer.

"I didn't think so."

I thought it better if I continued to do the speaking. "I know this is a little strange, ma'am, but do you know your name?"

She shook her head.

I nodded mine. "I guess we're all in the same boat." I cringed at my own words. *Of course we're all in the same boat—literally.* "What I mean is, we're all facing the same problem. May I come up the stairs?"

"I don't own the ship. You can climb any stairs you want."

"Thanks." Grumpy and I climbed the treads. I held out my hand for a friendly shake. The woman looked at it like I had leprosy. I lowered my hand.

She studied me a little more. "Wow, you're built like a tank, aren't you? I assume the most expensive bill in your house is the one from the grocery store."

"I've never been to a grocery store that sent bills. At least I don't think I have."

"What's going on here?" she asked. "I want to know what you know."

I guessed her to be a little older than me, but not by many years. She was pretty in her own way and came loaded with attitude. I told her what little I knew, what we had been doing, and finished with the ghoul in the corridor.

"Didn't see no ghoul. I've been up here for a while, but I was in a room before…I don't know how to describe it."

"Before you were miraculously transported someplace else." Grumpy smiled. I could see the smile because the woman blasted him in the face with the beam from her flashlight.

"Yeah, somethin' like that."

Grumpy turned to me. "Hey look, Big Guy, there is someone on a deck you already checked. It appears that I was right—again."

The woman looked at me. "You're a big guy, why haven't you squashed this jerk yet?"

"I've been wondering the same thing. It just doesn't seem to fit who I am—whoever that might be."

"Well, if you ever change your mind," she said, "let me know. I'll lend you a hand."

Grumpy snickered. "You don't scare me, lady."

She turned and closed the yard that separated them in one stride. I could tell she had no respect for personal space because her nose was an inch from his. "Really? And here I was thinkin' you at least had some brains." The words were cold enough to give me a chill.

Grumpy backpedaled. "Ease up, woman. I'm not your enemy."

"Yeah? We'll see about that."

Grumpy looked at me and all I could do was shrug. I managed not to laugh and that was no easy task. Truth be told, I started to feel sorry for the guy.

Several unusually long seconds passed before the black lady stepped away. She seemed to soften as she moved a few steps down the corridor and stopped to study one of the walls. I moved in her direction and shone my light on the wall. We had some light from a window at the junction of hallway and stair landing, but I wouldn't want to try and read a comic book in it.

My light revealed a series of drawings on the walls. They reminded me a little of those wall drawings in Egypt—hieroglyphs. Yeah, that was it: like hieroglyphs in a pyramid. "You do this?"

"Yep, but I don't know why." She extended a hand to touch one of the sketches. It was the image of a boy. The kid looked like he was maybe ten years old. I don't know how much a man can glean from watching someone touch something, but I got the distinct impression that she was feeling a strong emotion. If I had to guess, I would say she gave it a loving touch.

At the base of the wall were several pencils and pens. A quick look at the number of drawings made me think that she had been at this for some time, but that didn't make sense. I had been in this hallway not all that long ago and she wasn't here. That meant she was fast, and to be that fast meant she had been drawing stuff most of her life.

Grumpy joined us but stood on my left with the woman on my right. I guess I make a pretty good obstacle.

I tried to take in all of what I was seeing on the wall: a boy, a woman, a house, what looked like the exterior of a school or an institution, a few people and animals without eyes—that creeped me out—and some sharped toothed monsters. There was a tall, scary looking man similar to what we had seen a short time before.

I also saw the figure of a very normal looking man. There was enough detail to make me think he was older than us. He looked confident, proud, and a little superior.

Nearby that sketch was another of a woman and superimposed over that was the image of a girl. They looked an awful lot alike, as if the woman was the little girl all grown up. There was a spooky mansion and even a pirate ship.

"It looks like you had a few things on your mind," I said.

"Maybe. I don't know." All the bluster had gone from her voice. She touched the old man image then moved back to the boy.

"What's that?" Grumpy pointed at what I first assumed was a basketball but under my flashlight beam I could see it was some kinda mechanical sphere. She had drawn it so that it looked like it was flying.

"I don't know. I don't know what any of this means." Her voice trembled a little. "I just had to draw the images. They're important."

"Important how?" Grumpy spoke softly, a skill I didn't know he had.

She put a hand to her mouth. "I don't know. I keep askin' myself that question but I come up empty every time. Why can't I remember? Why? Why? Why?"

I put a hand on her shoulder, slightly afraid I'd pull back a stump. She allowed it. "We'll figure it out."

She drew a hand under one eye. "You really believe that?"

"Yes. I choose to believe that. Believin' otherwise won't help."

"They look like tattoos." Grumpy leaned closer to one of the drawings. "These are pretty good. You show some real talent—"

He snapped up straight.

I had to ask. "What?"

"You did all of these?" Grumpy sounded a lot less cocky.

"Yes."

"Every one of them? There were no drawings here before you began defacing the walls?"

"Watch it, pretty boy." Anger had replaced the woman's softer moment.

"Not everything is a confrontation, lady. Answer the question. Were there drawings on this wall before you started drawing?"

"The wall was blank, I tell you."

Time for me to speak up. "What are you getting at, Grumpy?"

He pointed at one of the images I hadn't seen before, and I coulda swore his hand shook a bit. I looked to the spot on the wall where he was pointing. I saw it: a dragon. I moved my eyes from the wall to Grumpy's arm where the same tattoo glared back at me. The woman saw it.

I don't know what I expected. A gasp? A cry of surprise? A question? An accusation? Instead she swore. I don't mean she let slip a bad word. No sir, she spit out curses like a machine gun spits out bullets.

Grumpy appeared stunned, but managed to move down the wall. I walked with him, shining my light on scores of sketches. At one, he stopped, stifled a scream, backpedaled to the other side of the hall, then dropped to the floor. He pointed a finger that looked like it had palsy. He could barely speak. I had a feeling I had seen terror before, and this was it.

I redirected my light to the drawn image of an old man; a man with the devil's own smile, and hatred in his eyes. I don't know how the woman did it, but I could have sworn the evil image moved.

"Run! RUN!"

A woman's voice rolled down the corridor. I glanced to the far end and saw a young woman with wild red hair speed around the corner of the T-intersection of corridors.

We stared at her as she sprinted toward us. "This isn't a drill, people. Run!"

All this would be strange in anyone's book, but what I saw next kicked strangeness up a notch. Not far behind the woman was one of those flying basketballs I had seen on the wall. It carried too much speed and slammed into the corridor wall. It slowed for a second or two, then picked up the chase again.

I grabbed Grumpy's collar and lifted him to his feet. "Go. Get."

He didn't argue. The redhead shot past us and he was right on her heels. The wall artist was on the move, too.

I decided on a different approach. I might be able to outrun the thing, but sooner or later it would run us down. So I ran—straight at it. When I was in tackling distance I leapt forward, arms out wide and tried to take the thing down.

There was a flash and I landed face down on a hard floor.

The carpet was gone.

The hallway was gone.

The people were gone.

I was alone in a wide room. A glance around told me what I suspected to be true: the ship had shuffled again.

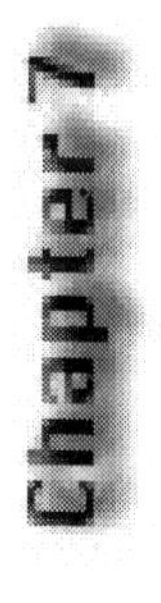

PUTTING HEADS TOGETHER

I PUSHED TO my feet and took a quick look around for that globe thing, that—sphere. I didn't see it. "Thank God." I took another look around. No ghouls either. All I saw was the wide, raised wood floor I stood on, a bunch of rows of padded seats, and some musical instruments on stands. There was also a drum kit.

The light was dim—nothing new there—so seeing detail was tough. Still, enough light pushed through partially open curtains along one wall. The curtains looked heavy and thick. It all made sense: I was in a theater of some sort. Didn't cruise ships have a place where bands played or entertainment personnel put on shows? I was pretty sure they did and this last shuffle had dropped me center stage.

The nausea I had felt the first time I was teleported or whatever you call it came back with a vengeance. I had been a little too frightened when I first hit the floor to notice anything but my heart pounding like an airplane piston. With no sight of the flying metal basketball thing, my belly decided it was safe to complain in the only way it knew how.

I sat on the stage for a moment, then lay on my back. A few minutes of slow, easy breathing calmed the storm in my stomach. I tried closing my eyes, but I was afraid I'd open them and see the hallway critter drooling on my face. That did nothing to soothe me.

Fortunately, I was very much alone and I'll admit—for a few moments if felt very, very good.

Once I knew my stomach was settled enough not to embarrass me again, I sat up. "What to do now?" I had no answers for myself, but sitting around waiting for something to happen didn't seem all that wise. I rose and walked to the windows, most of which were shrouded with heavy curtains. I figured that curtains were needed to darken the place for whatever kinda shows they put on in here.

I glanced back over the seating and guessed that the place could hold maybe five hundred folks or so. It kinda reminded me of a church, but with more comfortable chairs. Dim as the room was, I was able to make out two pair of double doors on the far wall.

I turned back to the window and stared out. A face was staring back in. I let out a whoop and jumped back. A hand that I assumed belonged to the face waved. The face smiled.

"Grumpy!"

He held up a finger then disappeared. Two other bodies passed by the window: a black woman and a redhead. It appears they had found each other after the shuffle.

"Big Guy!" Grumpy was all smiles as he entered the theater through a pair of double doors. "Did you miss me?" He came to a sudden stop and held out his arms to hold back the women. "You didn't… I mean…" He studied the floor.

"No. Not this time."

"What are you goin' on about?" The artist pushed past him.

"Turns out, Big Guy here has a sensitive tummy. Last shift, he puked his guts up. You should've seen it. It was amazing. A guy his size—"

"We get the picture." The red head glanced around the room like she was scanning it for clues. She looked at me. "You okay?"

"Yep. Thanks. You?"

"Peachy. Ended up in the men's bathroom. Never been in a men's bathroom. Don't want to go back, either."

I looked at the graffiti artist. She shrugged. "Kitchen."

It was Grumpy's turn. "Atrium, I guess you'd call it. Skylights. Wide room where people can gather and move around."

Red had a question: "Exactly where did you end up?"

I thought I had answered that. "Like I said. I ended up here. Well, specifically, I ended up in about the middle of the stage."

"Interesting."

"What's interesting, Red?"

She glared at him. "My name's not Red."

"Okay, what is it?"

She inhaled deeply and exhaled loudly. "You got me there."

"We gotta have some kind of name." Grumpy looked from person to person as if seeking agreement. "I mean, we can't keep saying, 'Hey, you.'"

Grumpy stepped next to me and faced the women. "Look, I call him Big Guy. Why? Because he's a big guy. Get it?"

"Don't patronize us," Red said.

"Fine. He's Big Guy. I'm Spartacus—"

"I've been calling him Grumpy." I tried not to smile when I said it.

"I don't deserve that name. I want a new one."

"Okay," the hall artist said. "We got Big Guy, Grumpy, Red, and me. Maybe you should call me Queen of Sheba."

Grumpy laughed, his voice echoing in the theater. The laugh stopped abruptly when the woman slugged him in the arm. Grumpy screamed, "Ow," then followed that with some very sour language. "What's with you, woman? You some kind of female ninja? Man, that hurt." He raised his hand and wiggled his fingers. "I can't feel my hand."

"Just for the record, gentlemen," Red said. "If push comes to shove, I'm with her."

"Me too," I said.

Grumpy made the kinda face a man makes when he's just guzzled sour milk. "Once again, it's the good looking guy against everyone else."

"Sketch," the artist said. "I was sketching when I first heard you guys. I can live with Sketch, but the first one that calls me Sketchy gets a pencil up the nose."

I believed her.

Red tugged at her hair. "You guys have a little more history together. That makes me the odd person out."

"We haven't spent much time together. We just met Sketch." I glanced at Grumpy. "We met not more than an hour or so ago, I'm guessing. Time seems different in this place."

Red chewed her lower lip for a minute. "I have a question for you, Big Guy."

"Shoot."

"Were you right behind us when we were running?"

"No. I ran the other way."

Red raised an eyebrow. "It was in a hallway. Are you saying you ran toward the sphere?"

"I guess so."

"You're not guessing, Big Guy," Red said. "That's exactly what you did. Why would you do that?"

I shrugged. "At the time it seemed the right thing to do. Doesn't matter. We shuffled before I could reach it—or it could reach me. Whatever."

"Interesting." Red looked at the floor as if someone had spilled a bag full of answers there. She looked at Sketch. "And they found you drawing?"

"On the wall." Grumpy was still rubbing his shoulder. "Really, who draws on a wall?"

Sketch took a step toward him and Grumpy took three steps back.

"I need to see those drawings." Red started for the door, then stopped. "Well, you guys coming or not?"

"Hang on," I said. I jogged to one of the walls next to the door and found a metal case set in the wall. The case held a fire extinguisher and a fire ax. I helped myself to the ax. I lifted it for others to see. "Just in case one of those flying balls comes looking for us again. I want to give it something to remember us by."

A PICTURE IS WORTH A THOUSAND WORDS

I LED THE WAY, the others behind me. I had convinced Grumpy to take up the rear. He was antsy enough to be an alert rear guard, always glancing over his shoulder. That's what we needed at the moment. I searched the corridor looking down connecting corridors to be certain seven-foot tall ghouls weren't having a card came with flying spheres. All was clear. For the moment.

We made our way out of the theater and down

stairways until we were on the deck where Sketch had been defacing the wall. *Defacing* might be the wrong word. There might be something to those wall tattoos.

Red wasted no time studying Sketch's graffiti. We found and made use of more flashlights. The corridor wasn't pitch black, but it was pretty dim.

While Red gazed at the drawings, I gazed at Red. There was something about her and I couldn't deny feeling some emotion for the red-headed woman. I didn't know why. If she felt any kind or warmth for me, she kept it under wraps.

"How long did it take you to do this?" Red kept her eyes on the wall. It looked to me like she was sucking in each image like a Hoover sucks up dirt.

Sketch shrugged. "I don't know. I seem to have lost my sense of time. Maybe an hour. Maybe two. For all I know, I was up all night making this mess."

"That couldn't be," I said. "I've been up and down the corridor a couple of times and I didn't see you."

"Maybe." Grumpy didn't seem convinced. "Remember, this ship shuffles. Maybe it does more than move us, it moves the decks and rooms too. This deck might have been higher or lower than it is now."

I wanted that to be a stupid idea, but I couldn't come up with any argument that would prove him wrong.

"Can't be much lower," I said. "The deeper we go into the ship, the less light there is. She had to have some kinda light to see what she was doing."

"Maybe," Grumpy repeated.

Red looked my direction. "Do any of these images mean anything to you?"

"Sorry, no."

She posed the same question to Grumpy. "Nah."

I cleared my throat.

Grumpy gave one of those theatrical sighs that people use to show annoyance. "Okay, a couple of them make me feel something. You know, a little emotional twinge."

"Why do I feel you're holding back something?"

He shrugged for effect. "Beats me. Maybe it's your time of the—"

Sketch pivoted and raised a finger as if it were a knife. "So help me, if you finish that line I will drag your skinny butt up the stairs and throw you overboard, and I'll be smiling the whole time."

She was loud. Her words were hot. And she scared me a good bit. It was a little hard to tell in the dim light, but Grumpy seemed to shrink by a few inches and his face turned pale.

Grumpy, to his credit, used his brain and took a step back, hands held at half-mast. "Okay, okay, I'm sorry. This whole thing has me off my game."

Red cocked her head. "You can remember your *game*?"

Girl doesn't miss a trick.

"No, I just meant… I'm gonna shut up now."

"Before you do," Red pressed, "tell me what you meant by a *twinge*."

"Most of these seem somewhat familiar. Some more so than others. And there's one—" He pointed down the hall to the spot where he had crumpled to the deck. "There's one down there that frightens me."

"Show me," Red said.

"I'd rather not."

"Show her," Sketch said.

He moved the few steps that would take him to the image that undid him. I noticed he walked near the opposite wall, as if a coupla feet of distance would protect him. He pointed.

The image of the old man with the horrible grin and evil eyes stared back at us. The hair on my arm stood up.

"This?" Red pointed.

"Yeah ...that's it."

Red put her face close to the drawing and shone her light on it. "Ugly cuss."

"You should have known him when he was alive." Grumpy's tone was softer than usual.

"You know who this is?" Red straightened and turned her gaze on Grumpy.

"He's my old man."

"And you're afraid of him?"

"If you knew him, you'd be afraid too. He was a monster."

"Interesting," Red said.

"I don't think so." Grumpy kept his back to the opposite wall.

"You don't get it." Red stepped to the center of the corridor. "Does anyone else remember their father? Or mother? Or pet dog?"

I said, "No." So did Sketch. Red admitted she couldn't remember any family members. She felt sure she had them, but she couldn't summon a name or conjure up a face.

"Why is it, Grumpy," Red said, "that you can remember your father?"

"You don't forget an animal like that," he said.

"Could it be because his dad is dead?" I wasn't sure that had any bearing but it was all I could muster.

Red thought for a few moments. "I want to say no, but I don't have a clue. I'm just trying to find a pattern. You know, make connections."

A couple moments of silence filled the space between us.

"I have an idea." Red moved back to the bulk of the sketches. "Gather round. I want to try something. Hold your questions until I'm done. Agreed?"

We agreed.

"Okay, I'm going to point at images at random. You tell me what you feel. Does the image make you feel good or bad; positive or negative. Clear?"

I had no idea where she was going with this, but she seemed like a pretty smart lady so I and the others went along with it.

"First, an easy one." She pointed at the drawing of the sphere thing.

"Bad." We said it in unison.

Next she pointed at a sketch of an eyeless man.

Again, "Bad."

She thrust a finger at odd drawing of a little girl superimposed over an adult woman. I hadn't noticed first time I saw it, but the little girl was barefoot.

"Good." Again, we were in agreement. I had more than a good feeling. I felt sadness, longing, maybe even a family kinda love.

The test continued. Red pointed at what looked like large, flying things that were human-like but had a stinging tail, at a man in some kinda cloak (that one kinda freaked me out), and critters that looked to be swimming in the air and had a head full of sharp teeth. That one made my stomach turn.

There were two special images. The first was the one of the old distinguished-looking guy. Red paused on that one, then touched it. "I feel like this guy is important. Very important." We all agreed with that. Then…

"Anybody feel like we should know the kid?"

I said yes. Sketch could only nod. She looked heartbroken. To my surprise, Grumpy seemed moved, too. Truth be told, I felt very strong emotions, positive emotions, when I looked at the image. There was love there.

"We have to find the kid," Red said. "I can't be sure, but I have a feeling he may be the key to everything. Him and this gentleman." She pointed at the old guy again.

I had a question for Sketch. "What made you draw all this?"

"I don't know. I kept seeing images and it seemed the right thing to do, like it's natural to me."

"That fits," Red said.

"Fits what?" I asked.

"I'm not sure yet. I'm starting to sense a pattern, but I need more time to percolate. My brain is still in first gear."

"Wow," I said, "if that's first gear, I can't wait to see fifth."

Grumpy cleared his throat to get our attention. "I have a suggestion. We should have a place to meet. I don't know how or why the decks shuffle, but we have to assume it's going to happen again. If we get scattered again, then we could all meet in the bridge. It's an easy place to find." He turned to Red. "If you want, I could hold your hand."

"I don't want." Red picked up the discarded pencils and pens. "Let's go where we have more light. I have another idea."

RED HAS IDEAS

RED IMPRESSED ME big time. She was smart and wasn't afraid to show it. I was going to have to defer to her in the brains department. Still, I couldn't figure out why she picked up the pencils and pens and carted them out of the corridor.

We went topside where the light was bright. Still gray, mind you, but brighter than what we had available in the corridors, even the ones with windows at their ends. I was glad for it. I needed a breath of fresh air, but the air never seemed fresh on this tub. For the first time I noticed that it smelled like day-old bread.

Red didn't lead us far once we got on the main deck. "I'm going to run off at the mouth for a minute. Just let me do it without interruption. We can discuss later. Okay?"

I saw no reason to disagree. "I'm good with that." Grumpy and Sketch just nodded.

"Good. That's good." Her eyes danced around as if reading something only she could see. "Here's what we've got so far. The best we can tell, we may be the only ones on this ship."

"We haven't searched the whole ship yet—"

Her head snapped up and she shot me a harsh glance. "I thought we agreed I wouldn't be interrupted."

"Yes," I said. "Right. Correct. Sorry. I didn't mean— This is me shutting up right now."

The corners of her mouth ticked up a notch. What a relief.

Again, she tilted her head down a few degrees and I could tell she was wandering the corridors of her mind.

"Big Guy is right, there might be more people to find. My gut tells me that at least one other person is onboard. The boy."

Sketch started to say something, but reigned it in. I had already come to the conclusion that very few things frightened her, so I had to conclude she was being polite.

"I can't be sure, but our response to the image makes me think we know the kid. I also think we know each other. Maybe we're friends, coworkers. I don't know, but we're all connected by something.

"We saw some strange images down there," Red continued, "but there's something stranger still—the fact that we didn't find the images strange. Okay, that's a lousy sentence, but you get my point. We should have been repulsed or, at very least, questioned Sketch's sanity, but we didn't. We accepted it all as if it was nothing new. Why is that?"

Red began to move her head back and forth like a metronome. The movement was subtle, but noticeable. She was weighing heavy thoughts.

"We each have amnesia. A specific kind of amnesia. There are a dozen or more types of amnesia. Most are caused by physical trauma or a disease like Alzheimer's. Our heads look to be in pretty good shape and it's doubtful we would all manifest the same form of amnesia at the same time or the same place. So, what does that leave?"

Grumpy took the question to mean the silence law had been lifted. "Drugs. Like what they use for some surgeries."

"Exactly. If we all had suffered some kind of injury, then we would be having problems remembering anything at all. As it is, we can't remember ourselves or our past, but we can still think, reason, communicate, and—this is a big *and*—we still have impressions. All of us responded to Sketch's drawings in the same way. We agreed on those images that represent something bad and those that represent something good."

"I think I'm falling in love with you," Grumpy said.

"If I'm lucky, I'll forget that comment too." Red got back on track. "Someone did this to us. I don't know why. Maybe we all know something that someone wants us to forget. That idea has problems.

It would've been easier to kill us than to get us on a ship like this. Missing. Too much missing stuff."

"Yeah," I said, "but you're making sense. Some knowledge is better than no knowledge at all."

"Why am I the only one who can remember his father?" Grumpy's tone sounded a little more civil than I had come to expect.

Red stared at him for a long moment, as if trying to decide if she should tell him what was on her mind. "Trauma. You're afraid of your father. That kind of lasting fear has to be rooted in something." She paused then spat it out. "He abused you when you were a child. Does that seem right?"

"I-I guess."

"I'm sorry to be so blunt, but I have a sense that things arc going to get worse before they get better. If they get better at all."

"No sweat," Grumpy said. I didn't believe him.

Red stepped to Sketch. "I need you—no *we* need you to do something." She handed her a pencil.

"Where? I don't have any paper."

"You don't need it. You've proven that." Red pointed at a wall behind Sketch. It was metal, but had a thick coat of grayish-white paint. "Think of the boy. Keep him in mind when you draw."

"Oh, come on." Grumpy's quiet moment had passed. "What do you think she is, some kind of psychic?"

"Yes, I do. *Psychic* might not be the right word, but she has some kind of gift. I'm guessing we all do. And don't ask. I don't know what they are. I'm working on impressions and patterns."

"Pattern-girl," Sketch said.

That sounded familiar.

Red cupped Sketch's face in her hands like they were old friends. "You can do this. The boy's life might be in danger. Go on. Give it a go."

She did.

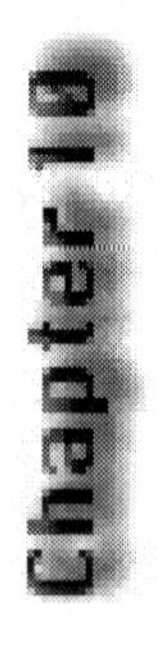

IN THE BELLY OF THE BEAST

FIRST, A BOY appeared, then came details of a room. Sketch was amazing to watch. Once the pencil started moving along the paint, she seemed to be a different person, fully absorbed by what was happening in front of her. It took only ten minutes for her to complete the task, and only one minute for the rest of us to say, "Engine room."

"I'll lead." I still had the fire ax and a flashlight. We had already seen a flying orb-sphere-basketball-thingy, a seven-foot-tall ghoul with big feet and a bad attitude, and Grumpy had seen his dead father. I had to assume that other creepy things waited for us. No one questioned my decision to take point. I guess it seemed as natural to them as it did to me.

We entered the innards of the ship and started down the stairs. Sketch's drawing showed enough detail for us to know that the kid was in the engine room, and the engines in the engine room drove propellers, and propellers were at the bottom of boats so...what little logic I possessed said to go into the belly of the beast.

We had descended as far as we could and, as luck would have it—or providence maybe—there was a handy-dandy sign with an arrow pointing the way: ENGINE ROOM.

We found the door to the room. It was big, made of steel, and reminded me of a bank vault door. It also had a large padlock and hasp.

"That's not good." Grumpy took a close look at the lock system. "The padlock and hasp are new. I doubt it's been open more than once or twice. No scratches, no aging. Yep, brand new. And worse, the hasps cover the screws that hold the backplate in place. It was designed that way, of course—"

"Everyone step back," I said. "Grumpy, keep your light on the lock."

"Sure, Big Guy, but you can't cut through hardened steel with a fire ax—Whoa!"

I raised the ax and brought it down like someone's life depended on it. For all I knew, it did. The sound of ax head impacting hasp assaulted my ears.

"Good try," Grumpy said. "But the lock is still—"

I let the ax fly again, this time putting all my weight into it. On the floor lay the lock, still attached to the hasp. I didn't break the lock or hasp, but I did break the screws that held it in place. Not my original goal, but I would take it.

Sketch started for the door, but I held out an arm and stopped her.

"He'll be scared," she said. "That was enough noise to wake up an entire town. So move it or lose it, Big Guy."

"Not yet. Let me go first." Part of my reasoning was to keep her safe; the bigger part was to shield her from the sight of a dead boy.

"Well, snap it up, or I'll find a new use for that ax."

I didn't doubt her for a minute.

I retrieved the flashlight I had set on the floor before I began destroying private property, took one deep breath, and opened the door. The engine room was black as a tomb. Not very welcoming. I plunged into the dark, casting my light around as I did. Inside sat engines, silent and still, safety rails, pipes and things that a non-mechanical guy like me can't name.

"Hey, little buddy. It's me. I think we might know each other."

Nothing.

"I've come to help. Sorry about all the noise."

"Tank?" The voice was tiny but strong.

"Is that you, buddy? We've been looking for you."

A kid I made out to be nine or ten appeared from a narrow space between two metal cabinets. I had the light in his face and he raised a hand to protect his eyes.

"Oh, sorry." I shone the light at my face. "Recognize me?" I expected him to say no.

"Of course."

He ran to me and threw his arms around my thick middle. Man, that felt good. It also felt familiar. I couldn't tell you how, but I knew this kid. I knew him well and loved him.

"Let's get outta here, kid. There's more people for you to meet."

When the boy saw Sketch, he broke into tears and ran to her. She dropped to a knee and pulled him into her embrace. The kid cried. Sketch cried. I might have cried a little, too.

"Mom. I was so worried."

I looked at Grumpy. "Mom?"

He shrugged. "It's the twenty-first century, man. After all we've seen and experienced so far, I'd say this is the least shocking."

"Let's get out of here," I said. "It's hard to fight in such an enclosed place."

Ten minutes later we were outside on the upper deck again. Everything looked pretty much as it did before except for the fog. It was closer and denser.

After the kid hugged everyone two or three times, he settled down enough to field a few questions. I took the lead with that, too.

"Okay, little buddy, strange question. What's your name?"

"You still can't remember?" He seemed bothered, but not hurt.

I shrugged. "Sorry, but no."

"I had memory problems too, but it didn't stick. I'm Daniel. You're Bjorn Christensen but everyone calls you Tank. You used to play football."

Grumpy snickered. "Bjorn." He snickered some more.

The sound drew Daniel's attention. "Your name is Chad Thorton. You're real smart. Mom calls you obnoxious because you are."

"You know how to make a guy feel good, don't ya, kid?"

Daniel ignored him and addressed Red. "You're cool and really smart, too."

"What's my name, sweetie?"

The kid didn't hesitate. "Andi Goldstein. We like to stay at your house in Florida."

"What about me, kiddo?" Sketch asked.

The question seemed to make him sad. "I call you Mom now, but your name is Brenda Barnick." He turned back to the rest of us. "She's a tattoo artist. And a really good one, too." Sadness covered his face. "She won't let me get a tattoo."

"You're just a kid." Even as I said that I knew I was wrong. He might be a kid, but he seemed a whole lot more.

Well, there it was. I was Tank, Grumpy was Chad, Sketch was Brenda, and Red was Andi. It was good to have real names.

The situation allowed me a moment to feel good; to feel like we were making progress.

Then Daniel screamed.

OUTSIDE AND EXPOSED

I SAW HIS EYES widen and his face go pale. It was the scream, however, that hurt me the most. I couldn't tell you how or when, but I had heard him scream like that before. Something about his back. Something was stinging him. The sound of it dredged up a whole lot of impressions. Not real memories, but the feeling that something bad had happened to the boy—to all of us.

I looked at his eyes, saw the direction he was looking, and turned to face whatever bogeyman was coming our way. I crouched, fist clinched into tight balls of flesh and bone.

No bogeyman. Just fog. Just gray, rolling, thick, smoke-like fog. And it terrified me.

Then I saw what the kid must have seen: something in the fog. Not just *in* the fog, but swimming in it like a person might swim in the ocean—only better, and faster. It was like watching dolphins swimming in the sea; dolphins with big heads, big mouths, sharp teeth and claws on the end of spindly arms. They looked hungry, fast and mean.

I stood welded to the deck. My brain refused to believe what I was seeing while my heart said I had dealt with these things in the past and it wasn't good.

"Inside!" Daniel was the one that said that. I tried to say it when I first caught a glimpse of those things, but my mouth wouldn't work.

"Everyone this way." I used the fire ax to point down the deck to where a door way led to the theater I had been in earlier.

No one argued with Daniel's advice or my direction. They ran next to the superstructure; I stayed between them and a fog that seemed to somehow gain speed. It was as if those things could move the fog bank at will.

It was only twenty or thirty feet to the doorway, but it seemed like a two-mile sprint. My heart was like a wild, captive animal trying to break free of a cage. I felt the chill of a cold sweat and I had to remind myself to breathe. This was industrial-strength fear.

A glance to the side revealed what I didn't want to see. The fog was closer and closing in on us at an unbelievable rate.

It was twenty feet out.

Fifteen feet.

It was at the railing. A hideous corpse-like face poked out of the wall of fog. I swear it was smiling or leering. It had the expression of a starving man looking at a plate of steak and potatoes.

The fog poured over the rail.

"Faster!" My voice rebounded off the fog on the one side and the metal wall on the other. Don't ask me to explain that. I'm no physicist, and frankly I don't care.

Another face. Then three. Five. Twenty. The wall of fog turned into a sneering mass of faces, each chomping at the air.

One face disappeared, then reappeared followed by its stringy body. It was headed for Andi.

She screamed. I yelled and put on the breaks. The thing was graceful in the fog, but outside the fog it was more like a trout flopping around in a rowboat.

That was a mistake on my part. It couldn't swim in simple air. I guess it needed the fog for that, but the thing could scramble pretty good.

It grunted, snapped, and headed for Andi.

I had the ax.

I used it.

I doubted killing things is my style. Guilt filled me as I put the ax in motion, but there was no time for self-reflection—even if I could remember more of my past. I made an appointment to talk all this over with myself when we reached safety. If we were ever safe.

The ax did its job. It was like hitting a cantaloupe. The creature's bold choice to leave the safety of the fog hadn't worked out like it planned, but that didn't stop others from trying. They might be fearsome, but they weren't any too smart. Each one that sprang from the fog hit the deck pretty hard. That would all change in about thirty seconds because the fog had just passed the rail. Only five feet or so separated us from it and the horrors it held.

One of the overly eager critters leapt from the deck and reached for Daniel. It caught the kid by the collar, but his claws missed any flesh. Daniel screamed that scream again and the coals of anger and fear in me burst into flame.

I bolted that way, then heard another scream. Not one of fear, but fury. A woman's voice. An angry mother's kind of scream. Brenda had the creature by the back of the neck and yanked it off Daniel before it could bring claw or tooth to bear. Then Brenda slammed the thing face-first into the deck. I knew she was furious because she slammed its head several times to drive home the point.

It stopped moving. I glanced back to the other creatures and saw those on the deck back up a few feet. I don't think they've ever seen anyone like Brenda do in one of their own.

Their caution evaporated a moment later. Short memories, I guess. The momentary pause was all we needed. I sprinted to the one closest to our party and gave it a sample of my shoe. It felt like I had kicked a ragdoll. It flew down the deck like one.

"Get in. Get in." Grumpy—Chad—had reached the door and opened it. The guy was full of surprises. I had him pegged to be one of those guys who scream like a little girl and do everything they can to save themselves.

I couldn't have been more wrong. He held the door open, held it in its place with his shoulder, turned to the mass of hungry murderers and tensed like a man about to take on a barroom full of bikers.

Daniel crossed the threshold first, followed by Brenda, then Andi.

"Move it, Tank."

I didn't need the encouragement. The moment I was through the door I spun back to the opening, grabbed Chad by the back of his shirt and yanked. He stumbled in and I grabbed the knob and pulled the door shut, but not before one of the little monsters got his grubby mitt between the door and the jamb. I closed it anyway. I closed it hard, putting all my weight and strength behind it.

A scream came from the other side of the door. I don't know if it was a scream of anger, frustration, or immense pain. I didn't spend much time thinking about it.

"Into the theater." Chad was again holding open a door. "Bring the ax."

I did and plunged past him. The door he held open was one of two. The entrance to the theater was through the set of double doors I had seen my first time in the room.

"Thanks," I said.

"Save it. Those things might figure out how to open a door." He was leaning back, a hand on each U-shaped handle. "Use the ax."

"You want me to chop—"

"No. Put the ax handle through the door handles. We need to barricade these."

I did as he said. After all, it was a good idea.

We checked for other doors, found the other pair of double entrance/exit doors, and used one of the metal cymbal stands from the drum kit to keep those doors from opening out.

A brief thought occurred to me. "You'd think they would have a way to lock these doors until they were ready to let people in."

"There are a lot of things about this ship that are off. That's the least egregious."

"Something else I can't argue with." I moved to the windows. I did so because I thought it was wise. I really had no desire to look outside.

The windows were covered with thick curtains to keep out the sun during performances and maybe to keep passengers from peering in. Chad joined me. The women and Daniel had moved as far from the doors as possible.

Deep breath, then I pulled the curtain back. A mass of milky-white faces was pressed against the glass. So many ugly faces.

They were *licking* the window. I closed the curtains and bent over, resting my hands on my knees.

"You going to hurl again?" Since it was Chad speaking I expected a little more mockery, but he sounded almost concerned.

"Nah. I'm just trying to—I don't know. I just need a moment."

When I straightened I got a good look in Chad's eyes. There was fear, but there was something else.

"You did good out there, Tank. You saved a life or two. Maybe all our lives."

"You done good too, buddy, holding that door and all. You're quick on your feet." I slapped him on the shoulder.

The girls and Daniel were seated on the floor of the stage. Brenda held Daniel like she was afraid he'd run away.

We walked to where they were seated.

Brenda looked up. "Now what?"

I had no idea what to tell her.

Then she—all of them—were gone.

BACK IN THE CLOSET

LAST TIME I got shuffled I ended up on the stage of the ship's small theater. Before that, I landed on the main deck where I left a pool of biology, something Chad hadn't let me forget. This time I was in a pitch- dark compartment.

"Swell. Jus' swell." I had landed on my fanny, which isn't all that comfortable for big guys like me. I put my arms out to my sides. The space was narrow. I couldn't extend my arms to their full span. I felt a wall on one side and something I took to be a shelf. I pushed myself up until I was standing.

Then I heard something. Something moving. Something shuffling. In the dark closet with me. I thought of the bogeyman we had seen in the corridor.

Worse, I thought of the fog creatures. Being stuck in a confined space with one or more of those couldn't be good. Not good at all.

"Who are you?" The voice was a tad timid but wore a veneer of bravery.

"Chad?"

"Is that a question or an answer?"

Yep, Chad. "It's me, Tank."

"Good to hear, Big Guy."

"Do you know where we are?" I wished for my flashlight. No telling where that was now.

"Oh, yeah, I know. I remember the smell." He sniffed. His voice was a little wonky.

That's when it hit me. "The closet?"

A sob. "Yes. Same closet." He wasn't hysterical, but he was zeroing in on it.

"Okay, okay. No problem." I took a breath. I was getting a little claustrophobic myself.

"I hate closets. I've spent way too much time in them."

"What does that mean?"

The sobs came in rapid succession. I was beginning to feel his panic. "My old man, moron. He used to lock me in closets. Sometimes for days at a time."

Before I could respond I felt his hands on my arms pushing me back. "I've got to get out of here. I'm losing my mind. You—you're breathing all my air." His voice softened. "Please, Daddy, I'll be good. I promise. I'll be good."

"Easy, Chad. I'll have us out in a couple o' moments. Just take a deep breath and—"

The punch hit me in the gut and it was hard enough to knock the air out of me. When I first met him we had tussled, so I knew he had decent strength, but the punch was harder than I thought him capable of. My stomach hurt, my head pounded, I was on edge, and I had had all I wanted of this ship. No way was I gonna let this guy wail on me.

I reached forward, felt cloth in my hand and guessed I had him by the front of the shirt, I pulled him forward then slammed him back. It sounded like I had just rammed the guy into some shelves. That had to hurt.

I clinched a fist, pulled it back. I had a good idea where his face was and I was gonna tenderize it. After setting my feet I started to let the punch fly.

But I didn't.

I stopped before my fist moved an inch. This wasn't right. I may not remember who I am, but this seemed way outta character for me. This was the second time I felt this. New emotions flooded my brain and my heart. Anger gave way to pity and a truckload of conviction landed on me.

I lowered my fist. "Ease up, Chad. Give me one minute and I'll have us outta here."

"Really?" Man, he could be snide. "How are you going to do that?"

"How did I get you out last time?"

"You're going to kick the door down from in here."

"You know something, Chad? For a smart guy, you can be really dumb." I reached forward and found the door, then ran my hand slowly down the side of it until I felt shredded bits of wood. "I don't need to kick anything down. The door is still broken."

The door swung open easily enough. "Viola!" I moved into the dim hall. A half-sec later, Chad was out of the closet and looked like a man who had just crawled free from a coffin.

He looked at me. "Um, listen. About what happened in there…"

"Forget about it."

"Maybe it could be our little secret—"

His eyes went wide and his mouth went slack. That could only mean one thing: something butt-ugly was standing behind me. I turned.

There are times when I hate being right.

A man stood behind me. Sorta a man. He was taller than me by a foot and a whole lot uglier. His face was misshaped, as if it had been made of wax and held under a hair dryer. He had a black mustache covering about half of his upper lip and one eye was twice the size of the other.

For a moment, I thought my heart had just given up and stopped. But since I didn't drop over dead, I figured it was still working some.

"No, Daddy. Please no. Leave me alone. Leave—"

Chad was on the run. I glanced his way, then looked back at the meanest dad I had ever seen. Except he had disappeared.

My brain lit on fire while my blood ran cold. If I weren't so terrified and worried, I mighta stopped to figure how that worked. I didn't take the time. An image splashed on my mind: Chad racing up the stairs and onto the main deck—the place where we saw a thick fog full of round-headed, sharp toothed monstrosities. That image was replaced with one of a dead, gutted Chad dead on the deck. He was outta of his mind with fear and I was the only one who knew what or who stood a chance of catching him.

I stopped thinking and started running. Running down the corridor to the spot where the big bogey man had been; running up the stairs where we found Brenda; running onto the deck where we had seen and barely escaped the creepies in the fog.

The door to the deck had just closed when I reached it. Then I did the dumbest thing in my life, I charged outside without a thought. It might have been brave, but it was also tempting fate. Maybe even tempting God.

I balled my fists so tight I could feel tendons strain against bone. I had no plan, no scheme, just a goal: find Chad and drag his fanny back inside before he became monster chow.

Three steps outside the door, I paused long enough to notice that the fog was gone and with it the infestation it carried. That was good. Everything was still a dull gray and I could see fog in the distance, but for now the fog-sharks wouldn't be jumping on deck anytime soon. Now I needed to find Chad before his terror drove him to do something stupid.

I asked God for help. I pleaded with God. I begged him. The prayer came naturally to me and felt familiar. Apparently, I was used to walking on hallowed ground.

Which way to go? I chose forward. We had walked that way earlier, so there was a chance Chad would choose the familiar.

My feet pounded the deck. My breathing came in great gulps. My mind ran to Andi and Brenda. Mostly it ran to Daniel. My fear felt like an animal with long tentacles was taking hold of my guts, my stomach, my heart and lungs. I could feel it moving, wriggling, churning.

Chad. Find Chad. Focus. Focus.

Most people paid little attention to me, once they got used to my size. I have never been the smartest guy in the room, but I have my insights and knew I could only chase down one lost sheep at a time. Still, I worried about the others.

The thing in my gut tugged at my innards some more. It was as if my fear had come alive.

No matter. I had my mission. I had my goal. Find that smart-mouthed, egotistical, chucklehead and save his bacon if I could. I might fail, but it wouldn't be for the lack of trying.

I pressed on, glancing into windows, looking up to the higher decks where I could, but no Chad. Then I reached the bow.

And there was Chad—straddling the safety rail that ran around the ship. Except here it wasn't a rail made of tubular steel. It was more of a parapet with a wood cap over a short steel wall.

A moment's relief. He was still alive. Then more tension and fear when I realized he wasn't taking a break but giving some serious thought to going over the edge.

I slowed to a walk, but continued forward. To my right was the wall that enclosed a room we hadn't been in.

"Chad. Dude. Whatcha doing? That doesn't look all that safe."

He ignored me. He didn't even bother to look at me. Something else held his attention. I reached the open deck of the bow and to my right stood the focus of Chad's attention: his father. Uglier than before and twice the size any man should be. One eye was now the size of a saucer and the other, although closer to the correct size for a guy standing twelve feet tall or so, oozed something milky-white. His face was even more twisted and his skin was almost see through. I could see things crawling just beneath the surface.

No wonder Chad was considering taking a dive. For a moment I considered doing a swan dive over the edge myself. If I could have put the guy down right then and there, he would still win. I'd be seeing him in every dream from now till heaven.

"Leave me alone, Dad. I haven't done anything to you. Why do you hate me? Why?" Chad broke into tears.

Dad raised a hand and pointed over the bow, encouraging Chad to jump.

"Look at me, Chad." I tried to sound calm although a hurricane of emotion raged within me.

Nothing.

"Chad!" My voice echoed off the hard surfaces and rolled over the water. "I said *look at me*."

He turned his face my direction. His expression nearly broke me. His face showed a lifetime of hurt, of pain, of rejection.

"Help me, Tank."

I could barely hear him. That's when I noticed the blood. It ran from his nose and a nasty cut on his right cheek and right half of his forehead. I noticed some blood on the one hand I could see. My guess: he had tripped while running and did a header into a bulkhead or into the deck.

Chad turned his attention to the ghoul he called *Dad*. Then he leaned a little more over the edge.

"Don't do it, Chad."

"It's the only way out. Death. Blackness. Nothingness. That's better than this."

"What if death isn't the end, Chad?"

He didn't respond other than tipping a few more inches toward certain death.

"Chad, I'm here. I'll stand by you. I'll stand with you. Just trust me."

"You'll stand against that?" He pointed at Dad. "No one can stand up to that."

I was lost for words. That thing could flatten me in a second if it had a mind to.

"Chad, if you go over, then so do I. No man should die alone. I'm gonna be with you on the deck or in the ocean. You are not alone. We are never alone."

His eyes drifted back to me. "I'm no good, Tank. I never have been. I'm a loser. I was born a loser. I'll die a loser. You don't like me. I've done nothing but antagonize you."

I nodded. "Yep. You're good at that. It's your super power."

"See?"

"What I see, buddy, is a man in the need of a friend. I'm that friend."

Tears trickled down his cheek. "What about him?" He nodded at Dad. "We can't stand up to that."

"Resist the devil and he will flee from you." I don't know where that came from, but it felt right.

"What?"

"Don't ask me. I can't even tell you how old I am." I looked at Ugly who was no longer content to point at the sea but was now gesturing for Chad to finish the job of killing himself.

Chad straightened on the rail. He was no longer leaning over the ocean.

I had had enough of standing around. I started toward Chad without giving a glance to Dad. If he wanted to kill me mid-step, I couldn't stop him. I resigned myself to death. Even that seemed familiar. I couldn't recall my past, but I guessed my life wasn't boring.

Chad eyes widened again. "What are you doing?"

"Resisting the devil, buddy. Just resisting the devil."

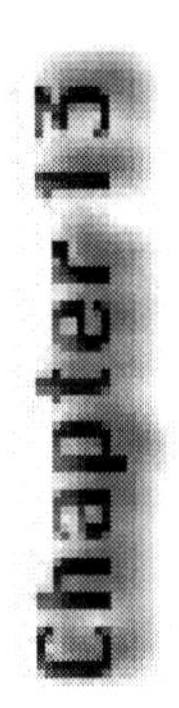

SHIFT, SHIFT, SHUFFLE

SEVERAL IDEAS RAN through my weary brain. I could rush Chad, grab him, and pull him onto the deck. Chancy. That struck me as a stupid idea. I'd do it if I had no choice, but instead I went with something less Hollywood. I held out my hand. "Come on down, Chad. You're giving me gray hair."

"What about him?" He nodded in the direction of Ugly.

I gave the ghoul a glance. "He will do what he will do. Even if he kills us, we will die on our own terms."

Chad thought about that for a moment and I thought about yanking him off the railing. I chose not to and prayed that I wouldn't regret it. Crawling off on his own would let him feel like he made the decision to live and hadn't been forced into it.

He took my hand and planted his feet on the deck. I took him in my arms to give him a manly bear hug, but then held him a little longer than was natural for me.

I felt a warmth in my body. The fear that had been tugging at my guts disappeared. My eyes stayed closed but I could tell we were covered in light.

"Um, Tank, this is a little awkward."

"Right. I don't know..." I stared at him. His wounds and the blood were gone. I couldn't tell where the cut on his cheek and forehead had been. I told him about it. He had been healed.

Dad let out a furious wail that could be heard a mile away.

"Oh, shut up," Chad said.

That made me laugh. I had no reason to laugh. I still didn't remember my past, was still on a dead ship adrift in the ocean, and the rest of our group was still missing. Sometimes, if people get frightened enough they laugh. Maybe that was me. I didn't have enough energy to care.

The giant bent at the waist and put his ugly mug close to our faces. He was real enough and his breath smelled like he had been lunching on raw skunk.

"Maybe we should run," I suggested. Not that I thought we'd make it.

Chad swallowed hard. "No way, Big Guy. I'm done running. If I'm going to die, it's going to be against my will, not because this thing forced me into suicide.

I began to question my sanity. After all I had seen, I probably should have done that sooner, but this brought the point home. I had to be nuts because Dad seemed to shrink some. Chad noticed that too.

"All my life, you have abused me in every way possible." Chad was getting hot under the collar. "I put up with it because I was too young to do anything about it. Well, I'm not a kid anymore. I don't have to put up with you for another minute."

Scary-Dad shrunk a little more. I remembered nothing of childhood, or for that matter, my adulthood, but Chad seemed to be dredging up horrible memories from his past. Maybe having amnesia was better.

"Go ahead, Dad. You're big and bad. Do something to me now. You might get away with it, but I won't give you the satisfaction of seeing me afraid again."

The incredible shrinking dad shrunk even more. It was as if it had been empowered by Chad's terror, but starved in the face of Chad's courage.

Chad must have put those two ideas together because he got louder and bolder. He let loose with a string of insults and curses that would have sent the sailors on this ship running, if there were any sailors on this ship.

Before my eyes what had been a deformed giant of a man reduced to normal size. He stepped back from Chad. I'm pretty sure I saw his swollen lip quiver.

Chad kept venting, and as the specter of his father diminished Chad's courage and intensity grew. Somehow, Chad's external injuries had been healed; no doubt his emotional injuries were being cured now.

The Dad ghoul grew smaller and smaller. When he reached the size of a child, he up and disappeared.

We stared at the spot where he had been standing.

"Okay," I said. "Now I've seen everything."

"You haven't seen anything." It was a new voice. An angry voice. A threatening voice.

A man in a red robe rounded the same corner I had and moved onto the bow deck. Dread filled me from toes to skull.

"Who—" I began.

Red Robe raised his hand.

He was holding something.

A gun?

No, it looked like a television remote control. He pressed a button.

Shift.

I stumbled down a half flight of stairs. I managed to stay upright, but my body lodged a serious protest in my knees, left ankle, and lower back. Still, I had to be thankful I didn't go head first down the metal treads. That would have been a good way to pick up a few dozen bruises, a broken bone or two, or even a busted neck.

It took me a moment to stop swaying. It was dark. Like I was locked inside a lightless vault. I wished for my flashlight. I had no idea where that was. It went missing. *Okay, I stumble down so if go back the same way I fell, I'll be moving up toward the light—*

Shift.

My nose hurt and for good reason. I was face down in the dark again. Judging by the pain in my head, I had landed face first on the steel floor.

I could smell oil. Oil and diesel. The engine room. Daniel had been locked in the engine—

Shift.

The theater again. At least this time I had a little light to judge my situation—

Shift.

A bed. Except I was crossways in it with my feet hanging off the side leaving me in a kneeling position. Some light through portholes. Gray. Large room. Nice. A white officer's style cap rested on a desk near the head of the bed. Captain's quarters?

Shift.

Kitchen.

Shift.

Flat on my back on top of the superstructure. Gray sky overhead. Gray horizon—

Shift.

Dark again. Standing. Stumbled back into what felt like shelves. A few touches later I judged that I was in a storage room for linens and towels.

Shift.

Cold. Metal all around. Smell of meat. Inside a large industrial refrigerator. I heard no compressors. Cold, but not freezing. No power.

Shuffle.

On my hands and knees. Puking again. Praying that this would stop. Dizzy. Unsteady. In pain. Ready to collapse. I raised my eyes enough to see I was out in the open again. I wretched a few times more. Someone else did the same. Then someone else. I wasn't alone.

I pushed back from the mess I made and sat on the deck, my arms around my knees, my head resting on those arms.

Breathe. Deep breath.

"Tank?"

I lifted my head and looked to my left. There was Red, Andi, with an impressive mess in front of her. "You okay?"

She cut her eyes at me. "Sure. Don't I look just swell?"

"No, but you're still beautiful." I eased myself down so I rested on my back. Man, I needed to rest.

"I bet you say that to all the vomiting girls." That was Brenda. She was behind me somewhere. I didn't bother looking. That would have meant moving and moving meant more yakking.

"Where's Daniel?" I asked Brenda.

"I'm here, Tank. I'm okay."

It was great to hear his voice. "I guess you tossed your cookies, too."

"Nah," the kid said. "I never throw up. That's for babies."

"Okay, buddy boy. I'm gonna tickle you until you turn purple."

He chuckled but I was pretty sure it was a courtesy laugh. "Bring it."

That gave me a reason to smile. "Okay. You free next week, 'cuz I'm gonna need a little time."

A shadow fell over me. As much of a shadow as a body could cast in the gray light. It was Chad.

"Hey Chad. I know, I know. I did it again."

"We all did, Tank."

"Not me," Daniel said.

I sat up and looked around. We were higher than the main deck and a few deck chairs were scattered around and few patio style tables. I worked myself to my feet. The deck was maybe twenty-five percent as long as the main deck. Rising from the middle of the deck was one of the ship's smoke stacks. No smoke. That was to be expected since we had been without power since I woke this morning, or afternoon, or whenever it was.

"Sun deck," Chad said.

The others joined us. Not to put too fine a point on it, we carried a bit of a stink with us.

I was tense. I kept waiting to blink and end up somewhere else in the ship. That didn't happen, but I hadn't wasted my worries. The guy in the red robe appeared at the top of the stairs, the stairs that led down to the next deck. Man, he looked familiar, and not in a good way. The robe was open in the front revealing an expensive looking three-piece suit. Like everything else, it was gray.

Daniel stepped behind me. Brenda was at his side, her hand on his shoulder. "Slick doesn't get close to Daniel. Got it, Tank? No matter what, Red Robe doesn't get within twenty feet of the boy."

"Yes, ma'am." That was all I could think of to say.

"I have had enough of you." Red Robe took two steps closer. I moved to the side to stay between Nutcase and Daniel.

"Yeah?" Chad said. "I don't even know you and I've had all I can take of your face."

Red Robe turned to stare at Chad. "True, we haven't met face to face yet, young Chad, but I know about you. I know all about you. You are a problem."

He turned to us and his eyes turned a glacial blue. *His eye color changed.* That seemed familiar, too. I was getting sick of hints about my past. I wanted real information.

"You all are a problem to us," Red Robe said. "And we will stand for it no longer."

"Us?" Andi said.

"The Gate." It was Daniel that answered. "Long story."

I hoped to hear it someday.

"And the kid. We hate you most of all, Daniel."

Brenda snarled. "One step closer, Slick, I'll separate your head from your body."

"Sure, you will." He didn't sound convinced. "I'm not afraid of a tattoo artist." He did take a step back. "I have something to show you. You, Brenda, and you, Chad, should enjoy this."

He raised the remote control in his right hand, gave us a sick grin and then, like some old time actor, shouted, "Behold."

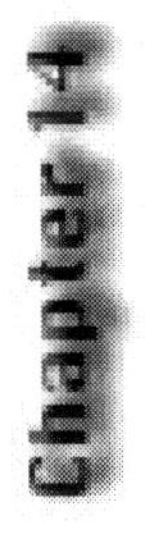

GRAY SKIES ARE GONNA CLEAR UP

THE MOMENT RED ROBE said, “Behold,” the gray skies went black, a black filled with funny lookin’ stars and other things I couldn’t quite figure out. One thing I *could* figure out: they were gettin’ closer and I didn’t have a good feeling about that.

“What the…” Chad said.

Then things got weird.

A hole appeared in the sky. Like someone took an ice pick and gave the heavens a good poke. The hole drew closer and grew bigger.

“Should we run?” Andi sounded a little on edge. If she hadn’t, I would have been worried. I was on edge. More than that. I was paralyzed with fear.

“Run where?” Brenda said. “There are creeps wherever we go.”

The hole turned into a tunnel. I could see down its middle. It reminded me of a long train tunnel, except it was rotating, expanding, and moving.

“Wait,” Brenda said. “I know this. I’ve seen this.” She pulled her eyes away from the thing in the sky and stared at Chad. “You. This has something to do with you, doesn’t it?”

Chad stood statue-still for a moment, not hearing, not moving, not responding. His mouth opened and I half-expected words to come out. No words came from him, but a gut wrenching, eardrum bustin’ scream did. He clamped his hands on the side of his head as if shutting his ears would make him blind to what was before his eyes. Of course, that makes no sense, but nothing on this ship made sense.

The ship rose. I mean that in the most literal way I can. The ship lifted out of the water. The deck heaved beneath our feet. Andi fell, Brenda stumbled, and I had to shuffle my feet several times to keep my balance. Oddly, Daniel seemed to ride the deck just fine. Youth.

The tunnel, the tube, whatever you want to call it, swallowed us whole. It swallowed the entire ship.

“Ain’t no way this is good.” It wasn’t profound, but my statement was accurate.

Brenda steadied herself and looked to be on the edge of panic. Daniel had said we all knew each other and I believed him, but I remembered so little. Still, I had the feeling that Brenda didn't scare easily, and seeing her terror made me even more afraid.

The ship moved through the tube bow first. Around us the tunnel spun. The wall seemed to move as if it were alive. Then I saw the first face. A frog-like face. A demonic face. It reminded me of one of those statues people used to attach to old gothic churches and buildings. Gargoyles. That was it. I was looking at the face of a butt-ugly gargoyle. It opened its mouth.

Then there was another, then another. The place was alive with them.

The ship began to flip over like it was capsizing in slow motion. That got our attention. Any moment we would slip from the deck and fall into the sides of the tunnel and become gargoyle food.

But we didn't. We turned over all right, but we didn't fall. It was as if there was no gravity. We just stayed in place.

I struggled to come up with a plan of action. I could probably reach Red Robe, but then what? I guessed we might need him to get back home, and if not home, a better place than this.

We emerged from the rotating tunnel into a black space filled with giant slowly spinning snowflakes. Each snowflake was large enough to hold a man. In fact, I saw people in them. Something else that made no sense.

"Look familiar, boy?" Red Robe moved close to Chad. "How about it? This is the place you visit when you do your remote viewing thing. Look around you, boy. You move yourself here when you do your astral projection thing, but you are a mere amateur. Nothing more. You wade in the shallows, Mr. Chad Trenton, while the Gate swims in the deep waters. Look, I moved a whole ship from one multi-verse to another many times and I can do it again."

He raised the remote control. "I can do all that and more. And if I want—and *I want*—I can move just myself and leave all of you right here. Alone. Helpless."

"Why?" Andi asked.

"Ah, the lovely Andi Goldstein. Always searching for answers and patterns and connections." His lips parted. "Because I want to, Ms. Goldstein. Because I can. Most of all, because I have grown weary of you and your friends destroying our work."

Over the bow I could see snow covered cliffs and a huge, black surface, like a wall.

"We don't even know who you are." Brenda added a colorful but not endearin' reference.

"Well, that's to be expected with the memory loss." The wicked smile came out again.

The ship shuddered and the space around us lightened a tick or two.

Red Robe continued, apparently enjoying his own voice. I missed his first few words because one of the giant snowflakes drifted close to the safety rail. It spun slowly on its axis. Inside were several children. Children with coal black eyes.

"…around you," Red Robe was saying. "This is your new home…"

Another snowflake drew close. Inside it was a swarm of "things." They were about the size of a child's doll and looked like small people but with large lumpy heads, spindly arms and legs, and leather skin. They also had skin-covered wings. Worse, they had tails equipped with nasty looking stingers.

A movement near the steps to the sun deck where we were caught my attention. I braced myself for more terror. Instead, a man in a suit slowly ascended the steps and moved onto our deck. He glanced at us and smiled. He was tall, had gray hair, and oozed intelligence. Of all the things I had seen since waking up on this ship, he seemed the most familiar.

The man moved slowly and silently. For some reason the snowflake with the black-eyed kids in it backed away. The one with the swarm of uglies in it stayed in place.

I don't know what the new arrival had in mind but I sensed he was on our side. To keep Red Robe's attention on us and not on the man he had yet to notice, I asked, "You're going to abandon us? What about Daniel? He's just a kid."

"Your good and kind heart, Tank, is what makes you stupid. I don't care if Daniel is a kid. Leaving him here will be the greatest joy of all. We have grown weary of all of you, but none more than Daniel. We hate him the most. You can't win. Not even with Daniel on your side."

"Excuse me, Dr. Trenton," the stranger said.

At least he was polite.

Red Robe—Trenton—turned sharply and got a face full of fist for his effort. The stranger put some weight into it. So much so, that Trenton's head snapped around and he dropped like a sack of rocks. Judging by the way his head bounced on the hard surface, I was pretty sure he was unconscious before he hit the deck. The remote he had been holding bounced a few times and skittered five or six feet away.

The stranger stood over the body like a heavyweight boxer over an opponent. Impressive. Then his mood changed. "Ow, ow, ow." He jumped around shaking his hand. "I didn't know punching someone could hurt so much."

"Professor!" Daniel raced from his protected spot behind me and threw his arms around the stranger. "Professor. I miss you so much."

The stranger embraced him like Daniel was his grandson. Brought a tear to my eye. Then he pulled away and retrieved the remote. "I hope this isn't broken. I hadn't thought about it being dropped. Stupid of me, really."

I looked at Andi, then Brenda, then Chad. Each shrugged. "Familiar?"

"Very," Andi said.

"Friendly good."

"Daniel thinks so," Brenda said.

The professor walked our way. He held his boxing hand a few inches from his side. It was swelling. No doubt there was a broken bone or two in that hand. Still, his mitt worked well enough to hold the remote.

"Who are you?" I asked. "I mean Daniel knows, but I don't have a clue."

"I'm a friend."

"He's the professor," Daniel said.

"Not now, son," the professor said to Daniel. "Our time is limited. You will all remember soon enough."

The snowflake with the swarm of toothy fairy things began to shake. Whatever they were, they wanted out.

He turned to Brenda. "Barnick, you are a royal pain." He leaned forward and kissed her forehead.

"Don't ever change." He set his good hand on Daniel's head. "Protect him. He's the key."

"Of course. I will."

The professor looked like a proud father.

The buzzing of wings and a hundred tiny screams came from the human-like bugs in the snowflake.

The professor turned to me. "Tank, you were right about everything. I was wrong. Thank you. Whatever you do, stay the course."

"I don't understand."

"I know." He gave me a sad lookin' smile. His eyes were extra moist. "I need you to remember something."

"I ain't been so good at remembering lately."

"You can remember this." He spoke loudly, no doubt hoping one of the others could recall what he said if I failed to remember. "Revelation 9:14–15." He paused, then, "Say it, Tank."

"Revelation 9:14–15."

"Good. Very good." The professor took a deep breath.

Chad stood in silence. I think it was the longest span of silence he had ever endured.

The professor held out the undamaged hand. Chad shook it. "I wish we could have worked together." He motioned to us. "These are your friends. Believe that. They will annoy you and try what little patience you have, but don't turn on them. They need you as much as you need them. You are not alone, son. You never have been."

Chad just nodded.

"Something else, young man. This will make no sense now, but it will soon. Losing something we have doesn't mean we're lost."

"I have no idea what you mean."

The professor didn't respond to that. He looked at the vibrating snowflake thing. It was bulging.

"We're almost out of time." The professor took a few steps back before speaking. "All you've been through, all the missions you've been on, all the dangers you've faced, have been for a reason. In a way, it's been training. Every battle, every skirmish, every threat has been a prelude to the war that must come. The war you must win."

Puddles formed in his eyes. I had puddles in my own.

"Have a good life; stay true to the mission. Your journey is not done. Heaven and Earth need you." He looked at Red Robe. "Trenton is not the one you're looking for. He's a flunky and nothing more. There is someone else you must find." Then he said a name: "Ambrosi Giacomo."

The name meant nothing to me.

"Come with us, Professor." Daniel was in tears. "Don't leave again. Please don't."

"I can't, son. Too much to do. Too much to learn. Too much to discover. I'll do my part wherever I am." He moved between us and the flying stingers. He lifted the remote. "I love you all. I always have."

The snowflake contraption gave way and the swarm emerged.

"Professor, look out!" I started for him.

Everything was gone.

ROCKING.

Like an infant in a cradle.

Gentle. Smooth. Even. Familiar.

I opened my eyes and saw the ceiling of my room. I sat up and hung my legs over the side of the bed. My feet were clad in dress shoes (scuffed up pretty good) and I still wore my tux. I hate tuxes.

I rubbed my face for a few moments and let the memories settle in. I'm not a drinker (made a few mistakes in the past) but I felt a little hung over or maybe drugged. I searched for my latest memory and it came to me easily. I was on a 1950s cruise ship sailing around the Gulf of Mexico on its last voyage. We had received invitations in the mail and it sounded like fun. And boy, did we need some fun together. We were getting on each other's nerves just hanging around our Dallas Hotel.

Someone knocked on my door. I could hear people talking in the hallway and outside. A bright sun poured light into the room.

"Just a sec."

I stepped in front of the mirror and took a good look at myself. My tux was worse for wear. It musta been a hard night.

I opened the door. Andi and Brenda stood before me, both in evening gowns which seemed entirely wrong for the time of day. But then again, I was in a tux. Daniel stood between them. Behind them moved a stream of passengers. For some reason, it struck me as a good thing to see. One of those passengers was Chad. Yep. He was in a tuxedo too, but no coat. He always was smarter than me.

"Hi, guys."

"We need to talk." Andi said.

"Did you have a dream, Big Guy?" Chad asked.

"Yeah. It was a doozy. The best part is I dreamed about the professor." It all came back to me in a tsunami of memory. "It wasn't a dream, was it?"

I stepped aside to let my friends enter. It was too many people in the small room but we could, at least, talk in private.

Andi sat on the edge of the bed, Brenda stood next to Daniel like they were tethered to each other. Chad leaned against the small desk.

"So it was all real," I said.

"Yeah," Chad said. "Every stinking minute of it." He hung his head like a scolded dog. "I'm a little embarrassed."

"Don't be." I stood in the middle of the room. "I wasn't at my best, either."

"You did great, Big Guy. Your big heart stayed true even when your memories abandoned you. I guess a psychologist would conclude that we are not the sum of our memories."

"As a man thinks in his heart so is he," I said. "It's a Bible verse."

Chad smirked. "Yeah, I kinda figured that."

Andi crossed her arms. She didn't have to say she was heartbroken. We had all seen the professor and now felt like we had lost him all over again.

"Speaking of Bible verses," Andi said, "what was that the professor gave you?"

"Revelation 9:14–15. You're right, it is a coupla verses from the last book in the New Testament." I stepped to a backpack I used for luggage and removed a Bible. I never travel without one. The others have teased me about it. There was no teasing now. I read the verses:

> "'Release the four angels who are bound at the great river Euphrates.' And the four angels, who had been prepared for the hour and day and month and year, were released, so that they would kill a third of mankind."

Brenda sighed. "I don't get it. What's that supposed to mean, Cowboy?"

"I think it means things are about to get serious. Real serious."

Preview of Harbingers 17

THROUGH A GLASS DARKLY

Bill Myers

"We will be arriving at Baghdad International Airport in approximately twenty minutes. Please return to your seats, stow your tray tables and put away any articles you may have removed during flight. Electronic devices must be turned off at this time."

I glanced up from my sketchpad and looked out the window. Nothing but brown. Brown hills, brown mountains, brown deserts. Same brown I'd seen the last two hours. I shook my head and went back to sketching.

The rest of the team, Cowboy, Andi, and Pretty Boy sat up in the other compartment, which was fine with me. We'd been on the outs since we got word of our little trip a couple nights back. I suppose you could blame me, but you gotta admit I had a pretty good argument.

It's not that I got somethin' against where we're heading ...'cept for the fact somebody's always blowing somebody up Iraq, Iran, or wherever we're goin'. I'm no geography major and don't care 'bout the details, but it's like every day you hear bad stuff happening here.

Not exactly the place to be dragging a kid, no matter how important our assignment. Then there's the stuff the professor told us when he dropped in for a guest appearance from that other universe or dimension or wherever he is:

"Every battle has been a prelude to the war
that must come. The war you must win."

Nope. Not with my boy. I don't care how much they guilt me. Daniel's my responsibility and I'm calling the shots.

My "discussion" with the others began two nights ago in that Dallas hotel, the one Chad scored for us as headquarters. I got no complaints about the place. But it don't give him the right to give orders, a fact that still hasn't registered in that egotistical brain of his.

It had been about 7:00 PM when our cell phones all lit up, all with the same instructions.

*Attached find e-ticket for your trip
to Iraq the day after tomorrow. Please
bring bathing suits.*

That's it. No name. No ID. Not that there had to be. We all knew it was from the Watchers, the little group of people, or whatever they are, who've been running us all over the place. Again, no complaints. Truth is, things were pretty boring 'til they came along. But this assignment, and with Daniel, well it was way over the top. And as we sat around Chad's living room, I couldn't of made it clearer.

And their response?

"You worry too much," Chad said, putting away another brew. "Ask me, you're smothering the kid."

"Smothering?" I felt my jaw tighten.

He nodded and belched. "Definitely time to cut the apron strings."

"Cut the apron—"

"If you ask me—"

"No one's asking you, Pretty Boy. Fact is, you're the last one I'd be asking."

"Which is your whole problem." He motioned to Andi, sitting at the computer and Cowboy who sat beside Daniel who was playing one of them cell phone games. "Before you guys met me, you were nothing– no plans, no organization, just stumbling around in the dark chasing your tails."

"Listen, you arrogant piece of—"

Andi coughed loudly. I glanced to her and swallowed back the words. I been doin' pretty good in the language department; tryin' real hard with Daniel around. But this jerk, he made it so–let's just say he knew how to push my vocab buttons. Particularly the blue ones.

"Guys, guys—" Cowboy (aka Tank) raised a meaty hand. As usual he was trying to be the peace maker.

"Not now," I said. "He may have you all fooled, getting this hotel and playin' his mind tricks." I turned back to Chad, "but you and me, we know different, don't we?"

He tried to hold my gaze but knew what I meant— the stuff I saw when we crossed through the portal together, when we entered that snow flake thing and I saw all those ugly pieces of his past life. Yeah, I knew the real Chad Thorton, top to bottom, and he knew I knew.

I continued. "Daniel, he's my responsibility and I'm done putting him in danger."

"Smother, smother, smother."

I swallowed, fighting back the impulse to rearrange his face. I'd done it before and he knew I could do it again.

"Your kid looks in pretty good shape to me," he said.

"And the scar in his back?" I said. "That fairy thing practically killed him."

Andi stepped in, nice and gentle. "But it didn't."

"This time."

Pretty Boy didn't let up. "The kid's got powers and gifts just like the rest of us. Not as developed as mine, no one's is, but the potential's there. And he was the only one who kept his head and didn't freak when we were on that Mexican dream ship."

"He's got a point, Miss Brenda," Cowboy said. "The Watchers put him on the team for some reason."

I motioned to the message on Andi's computer and on our cells. "There ain't no way in heaven or hell I'm letting him go to Iraq.

"Miss Bren—"

"People die over there, Cowboy. Every day."

"People die everywhere," Pretty Boy sighed.

"And the professor's words?" Cowboy said. "About Heaven and Earth needing us? And those angels chained under the Euphrates River?"

"Which, I might point out runs directly through the heart of Iraq," Chad added.

Time to go. I got to my feet. "Be sure to send me some selfies."

"Hold it," Chad said. "You're staying behind, too?"

"A boy needs his mother."

That's when everything got real quiet. No one ever turned down the Watchers before. And now that things were heatin' up . . .

"Maybe," Cowboy cleared his throat. "Maybe we should chew on it for the night. I mean it does sound kinda dangerous."

Chad snickered. "So Bible Boy is chickening out, too?"

"I didn't say—"

"You can sleep all you want," I said, "but there ain't no way I'm taking this child to Iraq. Come on, Daniel."

He got up and joined me, head still in his cell phone.

The plane lurched, pulling mc from my thoughts. I focused on the sketchpad. I was drawin' butterflies. I had them flyin' over a cool park with flowers and trees and a stream. Each one of them had an eye on each of their wings with all sorts of designs around them.

I shook my head over our recent conversation. It was true, I'd made up my mind about me and Daniel. There was no human way I would change it. Then again, with these little trips, we weren't always talking about *human*...

About Alton L. Gansky

Alton L. Gansky (Al) is the author of fifty works of book length fiction and none fiction. He has been a Christy Award finalist (*A Ship Possessed*) and an Angel Award winner (*Terminal Justice*) and recently received the ACFW award for best suspense/thriller for his work on *Fallen Angel.* He holds a BA and MA in biblical studies and was granted a Litt.D. He lives in central California with his wife.

www.altongansky.com

Made in the USA
Middletown, DE
29 October 2016